It did not matter if he hated her

The important thing was for him to go away. Never to come back.

Ryan's words were only a growl, hurled angrily toward her. "While I was waiting for you, were you with him?"

She stared back at him, afraid she could not make the lie work if her lips moved. His hands tightened on her arms. Hard. She welcomed the pain and tried to keep her eyes wide and blank.

"And the day before," he growled, "you were with me. In my arms. In my bed." She shivered, and he said grimly, "Naked, in my arms, loving with me." His voice sharpened and he shook her slightly, demanding, "Was he waiting for you while you were with me?"

VANESSA GRANT began writing her first romance when she was twelve years old. The novel foundered on page fifty, but Vanessa never forgot the magic of having a love story come to life. Although she went on to become an accountant and a college instructor, she never stopped writing, and in 1985 her first romance was published. Vanessa and her husband live in a log home on one of British Columbia's Gulf Islands.

Books by Vanessa Grant

HARLEQUIN PRESENTS
1322—SO MUCH FOR DREAMS
1386—ONE SECRET TOO MANY
1426—THE TOUCH OF LOVE
1490—ANGELA'S AFFAIR
1528—WITH STRINGS ATTACHED
1622—WHEN LOVE RETURNS

HARLEQUIN ROMANCE
2888—THE CHAUVINIST

Don't miss any of our special offers. Write to us at the following address for information on our newest releases.

Harlequin Reader Service
P.O. Box 1397, Buffalo, NY 14240
Canadian address: P.O. Box 603,
Fort Erie, Ont. L2A 5X3

VANESSA GRANT

Hidden Memories

Harlequin Books

TORONTO • NEW YORK • LONDON
AMSTERDAM • PARIS • SYDNEY • HAMBURG
STOCKHOLM • ATHENS • TOKYO • MILAN
MADRID • WARSAW • BUDAPEST • AUCKLAND

For Ann,
friend and holiday companion,
with love

ISBN 0-373-11670-5

HIDDEN MEMORIES

CHAPTER ONE

IT COULDN'T be him!

Abby had dreamed him in nightmares, memories suppressed and almost forgotten. A man's head and shoulders glimpsed across a room milling with art fanatics. Between them, the typical crowd of effusive, touchy women waving long cigarette holders and murmuring "dahling"; greasy-haired art students mouthing assessments of artworks they wished they could emulate. Hard to say which was the dream and which reality, but Abby had a years-old memory of moving through the crowd, dullness in her heart and her mind.

It had been raining. The dampness of a London drizzle had clung to her long blond hair, making it heavy and uncomfortable. She had gone to that London gallery. Looking for comfort, perhaps, as if standing among the paintings could make disaster come right again.

Two exhibits. Benedict's impressionistic clouds and waves downstairs. Upstairs, photographic images of harsh, shocking reality.

He had been watching, his dark eyes narrowed. Lean and strong, relaxed against the big marble post with a stillness that told her he would move at any instant. Dark hair, sun-bronzed skin. A stranger, and yet she had known him, his eyes watching across a London gallery. His exhibit. He was the only one who could have brought those harsh images of reality to life with camera and cleverness. In the memory, he had moved when their eyes locked. Very tall. She remembered looking up to meet his gaze. As tall as Ben.

And today——

Of course she would not recognize him after all this time. A dream from a place on the other side of the world. A shadow on her life. Not even reality. Except that sometimes she had woken in the night believing that the dream *was* reality!

She turned away abruptly, felt her arm imprisoned by soft, clinging fingers.

"Abby, dahling!" Heather Steinway's lips made a kissing motion toward Abby's cheek.

Abby tried to smile. "Heather——"

"Dahling, it's been so long!" Artificial fingernails dug into Abby's forearm through the sleeve of her blouse. "Up-island is no place for dahling Benedict's wife. You should be in Victoria, close to your friends. The people who love you." Heather flung her free hand out dramatically. "Today—such a significant event. Benedict would be honored. It should have come years ago."

Abby nodded agreement, knowing that honesty was not what this sort of event was about. Years ago, Ben's paintings would not have brought in enough to secure Trish's education—and no one but Trish could motivate Abby to go through the agony of this showing. Trish, and Benedict who had died too young.

Abby tried to shift away, but Heather's fingers clung more deeply. "Dahling, you simply must meet Thomas!"

Thomas looked like a hundred other art students. He glared at Abby with vacant eyes, his face ringed with longish, greasy hair. "Thomas has *talent*!" Heather announced. "You simply must——"

"Abby Stakeman! There you are!"

She turned toward the voice. If she could endure one more hour. She almost closed her eyes, picturing her small house on the waterfront. Peace. Quiet. She had not expected so many people today. Ben would have expected them. They had come because Benedict Stakeman's work was inspired, because he would never paint again.

Ben had always known greatness would come to him.

"Abby! Darling!"

Abby submitted to another almost-kiss, found her eyes moving to that spot where she had seen the man a moment ago. A man leaning against a pillar, near the entrance to the gallery. A lean, long man, watching with eyes narrowed. Of course it was not him.

In London, his eyes had changed when they locked on hers.

She tried to concentrate on the words flooding over her. Another woman, standing too close, head armored by a rigid helmet of blond hair.

"My dear, I know just how this retrospective must make you feel. All the memories!"

"Yes," Abby murmured.

Someone pressed a glass into her hand. She raised it to her lips. Too sweet. She disliked sweet wine. What *was* the woman's name? All the touching. All the people. Once it had been a game she shared with Benedict. Crowds of people. Women with too much money and too little reason for being. Critics. Hangers-on. Artists. Would-be-artists. Ben had loved it all, while Abby had been content to watch him accept the admiration.

She had been so young then, naively hero-worshiping the public image of the artist she had married, trying not to be disillusioned by the reality.

She saw the man again, a shockingly clear glimpse seen over the heads of strangers. Streaks of silver in his black hair. His eyes would be dark, always watching, narrowed.

Had he seen her?

Years ago, on the other side of the world...

Beside her, a voice demanded gruffly, "I want to know about that marvelous child of ours."

She jumped. "Hans! You startled me." She let out her indrawn breath, smiling up at the big, grizzled man beside her.

"Did I, my dear?" He chuckled. "One voice among all these?"

"Hans——" For an instant she had thought it was *him*, come to haunt her.

Ben's old friend swallowed her hand in his massive grip. She had always liked him, always been a little nervous of his overwhelming presence. The man was a legend, a painter even Ben had admired. It was Hans who had persuaded her that the time was right for this showing, time to bring the rest of Ben's paintings out of storage. Hans who had stood godfather and been there for Trish all these years.

"The child," he demanded with a rough gentleness. "Benedict's child. My godchild. She continues to show promise?"

"Trish..." Abby moved uncomfortably, knowing that lately her daughter was more interested in reading than painting.

"Not Trish," Hans said quietly. He was a massive man, his giant body crowned with a luxuriant mass of pure white hair. "Benedict would have wanted her name in full. Patricia Benita Stakeman." He pronounced the syllables slowly, with heavy significance.

For a second she could not answer. She knew better than anyone what Ben would have wanted. A son. Patrick Benedict Stakeman, to follow in his father's footsteps.

Abby shrugged Ben's memory away and said with a slight smile, "She insists on Trish. She's very stubborn about it."

Hans inclined his head, a gesture of tolerance. "She will be great, as her father was."

"Yes, of course."

Hans must have sensed some hesitancy in her voice. He said with strength, "She is the image of her father."

"Yes," Abby agreed. Patricia, at birth, a tiny form in her arms, dark curling hair and dark eyes that would later turn green. Such a contrast to Abby's fair skin and straight blond hair.

Hans waved toward the crowd that surrounded them. "You see, they have all come to pay homage to the artist. When can I see Patricia's work?"

"Trish is working with Callman. He says..." Abby shifted uneasily. Jean Jacques Callman had told her last week that he suspected Trish would never become a great painter.

A man she vaguely remembered touched her arm and said her name. She smiled a greeting. "That painting," he breathed. "The seascape!"

"Yes?" Abby had little hope of its selling. It was, she thought, so much like the seven others Ben had done that summer.

"I know just where he was coming from when he did that," the intense man whispered. "I can see it."

That painting. Waves on the beach. Benedict on the patio of a rented California beach house. She had stood behind him, staring at the blue-and-purple shades in the painted water on his canvas.

"What do you think?" Ben had asked. Smiling. Knowing her answer.

She never understood quite what had happened, except that the next time she knew better than to be impulsively honest. A great artist, but of course he had his faults.

Today she had done everything for him, although it was years too late. She had dressed in a pale blue suit that was almost identical to the one he had chosen for their wedding. Her fair hair was hanging straight and glossy down her back. He had liked it long and free, bleached by the sun. She half smiled, remembering. She had gone to the hairdresser for artificial sun when winter came. For Ben. She should have had her hair lightened for this showing. For Ben, because this was all for him. She pushed her hair back over her shoulder, shoving that old feeling of uneasiness away. Enough that she had worn the uncomfortable contact lenses today; surely the hair did not matter.

"What about my godchild?" demanded Hans when he had sent the whispering man away to make an offer on the seascape.

Trish would be eleven at Christmas; too young for the kind of pressure Hans wanted to put on her. Without her permission, Abby's eyes searched for the tall stranger.

"She should be here," Hans complained.

"She's got an art lesson today."

Hans frowned. "This should be the lesson. Callman may not be the right teacher for her." His pale blue eyes were passing over the heads around him. He was tall enough to look down on most of them.

Across the room, the stranger shifted. It was some trick of light and shade, a chance resemblance. In London his hair had been touching his collar softly, the unruly black streaked with premature strands of silver.

He had been too young for silver hairs. That day, he had worn a dark sweater that clung loosely to his wiry strength. Today, it might be the same sweater, hanging loose over a pale, expensive shirt. Dark hair. Dark eyes filled with life. Tall. Lean. You could describe him and make it sound as if the details were a catalog of Benedict Stakeman's appearance, although in reality Ben's personality had never made the kind of impact *he* could make.

And now...

"Abby, darling! So good to see you again!"

They all talked in exclamation marks, Abby realized with sudden weariness.

"Where have you been hiding? Wonderful, isn't it? All this. As if Benedict were alive still. I expect him to pop up in front of me any minute."

"So significant that he painted only in oils." The whisper was loud in her ear. "Group of Seven. Definitely."

One more hour. Just one more hour and she could go.

The man was a stranger, a trick resemblance. She glanced again, just as he turned away. No camera, she realized with sick relief. If it were him, there would surely be a camera slung over his shoulder.

Hans became tangled in conversation with someone intense. Abby moved, nodding and smiling and agreeing to it all. The touches, the soft voices. "Dahling, so significant...went to New York back in the beginning. That critic slaughtered Benedict. If the man were here today...another artist like Stakeman. Penetrating... the meaning of life in every stroke...oils are so much more *real*, don't you think..."

She saw her mother's natural gray hair over five heads of sprayed plastic. She had come to offer support, knowing how Abby dreaded this. Perhaps they could escape together, hide in a corner somewhere and pretend to be discussing true art. Abby suppressed a grin as her mother veered away from Heather's clinging grip and started talking to someone else.

* * *

"You look too real to be one of this crowd."

Ryan looked down at the middle-aged woman. "You're right," he agreed with amusement, taking in her soft gray hair, her slightly rumpled but tasteful pantsuit. He had a weakness for deep blue eyes on women of any age.

She whispered, "You're not a *significant person*, are you? I can't bear to talk to one more significant person."

They were at the edge of the room. He looked away from her, surveyed the faces and recognized the types. He knew that one or two had recognized him, but he had avoided them so far. It was a good thing there were no cameras allowed, he thought ironically. This crowd would come out of his developing bath looking brittle and phony. To the softly aging woman at his side, he said quietly, "They're only cardboard people."

"They make me feel like a stupid housewife." She laughed and shrugged. "Ah, well! I'm Sarah Rule."

"Ryan Marsdon," he offered, deciding that she had probably been talking to strangers confidently for all of her fifty-some years. "And I doubt you're a stupid anything."

She looked amused, not quite smiling as she asked, "Are you an artist?"

"Photographer."

"Talkative, aren't you?" She made the soft gray hair bounce.

He did not want to snub her gentle, innocent curiosity, although he was on holiday and had no desire to answer questions about his books or his nomadic life. He shrugged and said, "I just wandered in on impulse. Saw the sign."

She whispered, "It's by invitation only."

His lips twitched. "No one stopped me." In fact, the gallery manager had recognized Ryan, had shrugged away the lack of an invitation.

He saw her taking inventory, wondered what she saw. A long, lean man in a dark sweater and tailored pants. Immaculate. Expensive. Dark eyes. Dark hair streaked with gray. A harsh face, he knew, because he had been told he had grown into a hard man.

Curious, she persisted, "Why *did* you come?"

"I wandered through a Stakeman showing in London once." He shrugged. He was not about to talk about his personal ghost.

"You knew Benedict?" Sarah asked breathlessly.

"No." Habitually, Ryan turned Sarah's question back on herself. "You knew him?"

"Yes. Because of Abby. My daughter." His brows lifted and she shook her head in slight confusion. Ryan smiled, deciding that Sarah was the kind of motherly woman every lonely child wished for. Abby, he decided, had been lucky.

Belatedly, the name pulled strings of memory, old gossip. "Stakeman's widow?"

"Yes," she agreed quietly. He caught the echo of loss. "This is so hard for her," confided Sarah. "Seeing all these paintings again. She's had them in storage, you know."

Hard, thought Ryan wryly, collecting all that money.

"They were so much in love. He was so young. So tragic."

Soon Sarah would drift on, then Ryan would reclaim his camera from the manager and leave. He frowned at the closest of Stakeman's paintings. The man had been clever, copying a popular style, but Ryan had never been able to see much magic in Stakeman's work. He would not have come today, except that there had been a Stakeman showing downstairs from his own first exhibit.

It was years since he had searched gallery crowds. Looking for Gail always left him with that crazy emptiness. Memories. London. The image of wide, vulnerable eyes across a crowded room. A stranger, but he had recognized her as if she were close with the intimacy of old, shared lifetimes. He remembered that moment, moving toward her, feeling the certainty that this was what his life had been about. Waiting for this one woman.

How often had he lifted his camera to trap the significance of that elusive memory on film? For years, his gaze had caught on glimpses of memory. The sweep of a woman's shoulder. The incredible softness of an abundance of long blond hair. The impact of wide, deep blue eyes filled with mystery. Promises, masked by a curtain he could never quite penetrate.

Why the hell was he doing this to himself? Only moments ago he had glimpsed a profile that stopped his heartbeat. He knew better. Transient echoes of the memory. Never real.

"There she is!" hissed Sarah urgently. "Over there! Come on, Ryan. We'll pretend you're a buyer. That godawful Heather woman has her talons dug in. Come on! Help me rescue Abby."

Sarah caught his arm and he followed into the press of people. Anything to push back the old images.

"Abby, darling! You're the one to settle this argument. Tell me just how Benedict saw himself." The voice drilled painfully through Abby's brain. She held herself rigid as someone jostled against her back. A wall of people. They all looked the same, sounded the same.

"Settle it for us, Abby."

"Saw himself?" she repeated, and she could hear the high note of strain in her own voice. She had to get out of here.

"Yes. What did he aspire to? I think he always wanted to be another Monet. Graham, though, says it's the effect of Cézanne's landscapes that he really strove for."

She closed her eyes. Too many colors. Too many voices, most of them with no idea what they were saying.

"Another Monet," the voice repeated triumphantly. "Don't you agree that's how he saw himself?"

She felt her jaw going rigid. "He saw himself as Benedict Stakeman, not a copy of someone else." It was not completely true, she thought uncomfortably.

A gasp, almost a laugh. Abrupt silence, and she knew she should have said something neutral, putting them off. Then the voices rose up again to fill the uncomfortable silence.

Then her mother's welcome voice. "Abby, darling, you did shut him up, but you'd better get your breath. I've brought you a moment's escape."

Abby turned to her mother with relief, but she froze when she saw the man beside Sarah.

His face was older, more deeply lined. In London, he must have been in his mid-twenties. Now . . . she tried to lick her lips, but nothing would move. Tried to swallow, felt panic welling up.

"This is Ryan," offered her mother triumphantly. "Ryan Marsdon, who doesn't belong here either."

Abby tried to nod, swamped by an awareness of heat and summer and too many people. And that man, staring at her.

Sarah said cheerfully, "Ryan, talk to Abby. My daughter is going nuts with all these hangers-on."

"Abby?" His voice was a quiet challenge.

She tried to look away from him, but his gaze would not let her go. She felt herself cringe. He said quietly, "I could have sworn your name was Gail."

Abby gasped, "I—I have to find Hans Bunian." He knew it was a lie; she could see the knowledge in his hazel eyes.

She was caught, trapped between her mother and the man from her dreams. Someone said her name. Abby reached out for the voice, grasping for any interruption, any escape from the dark-haired stranger whose eyes were filled with knowledge.

Sarah turned and deflected the interruption with warm innocence.

Abby could not escape his gaze.

He demanded softly. "Why didn't you meet me the next day? Sunday?"

Had it been a Sunday? She shook her head, told herself that he was not real, just an image in an old dream.

"I waited," he said.

Hans's white head loomed on her horizon. She moved mechanically toward him, away from the man with silver lights in his black hair.

The stranger's hand touched her arm. "Gail..."

She felt the shock go right through her body.

She made herself hold his eyes, told herself there was only ice in hers. His eyes had been in her dreams, hazel turning dark as his gaze penetrated hers. A crowded London gallery, and she had known he could see everything about her in that first instant.

She said raggedly, "You're—mistaken. I'm *not* Gail."

He touched her arm and she felt the shock through her jacket.

She jerked away, said, "I'm Abby Stakeman. Not who you think I am..." Tightness welled up in her throat and forced the words out. "Whoever *you* are—I've never seen you before in my life."

It was a lie. Years ago in a quiet bookstore she had bought a book with his name on it. Had taken it home.

Had turned the glossy pages, picture plates that laid bare the heart of a country for the world. Had read the dedication.

Sometimes, in the dark places of her heart, she had dreamed that he would find her one day.

CHAPTER TWO

ABBY pulled the van over to the edge of the twisting highway just as Maple Bay came into view. She sat motionless for a moment, the engine ticking quietly, her hands loose on the steering wheel. The water spread out in front of her, white threads of wind on the blue of the bay, tall evergreen trees bending in the wind, marking the passage through to Georgia Strait.

Abby opened the door of the van just as a cold gust of wind twisted past. Quickly, she closed it again. All morning she had looked forward to stealing half an hour from her day to sketch the shore; but she would have to go home first, change into jeans and a thick sweater against the late September wind.

She was wearing a heavy blue cotton skirt with a light-weight matching long-sleeved blouse. Perfect clothes for work, for visiting her clients and working in the heated van, but too vulnerable for the wild autumn winds. She shrugged and decided it was not worth the hassle. For Abby, sketching was a way to let tension go, the ultimate contrast to her workday, but certainly not worth freezing in a cold September wind.

Perhaps she would do the sunset from her patio tonight.

She opened the window just enough to breathe in the fresh salt air. Automatically, her hands freed the silver clasp that imprisoned her hair at the nape of her neck. She twisted the hair back into place, catching the tendrils blown free by the wind. She almost decided to get out her sketchbook anyway then, but the van was firmly

18

associated with her workdays, not with play. The back was fitted out with computer and printer, drawers of files for her scattering of clients, a bench seat that doubled as a bed when she was traveling. As her mother had commented, if Abby had to make her living doing other people's books, at least computerized-accounting-on-wheels was more interesting than a dusty office.

Twice a month, Abby set out on a Monday morning and worked her way north on Vancouver Island, visiting her clients, doing their books on site, giving them printouts right there. Her clients were a scattering of solid little businesses between Maple Bay and Campbell River. Just enough to pay the bills, few enough that she was always back by Thursday night, ready for Trish's return from school on Friday afternoon.

She liked the feeling of being her own boss, the chance to stop between clients in interesting places and sketch her impressions. This week, though, four days on the road had seemed forever. Each night she had tossed restlessly in the narrow bed. Dreams. Too many dreams. The man from the gallery. That frightening moment of waking, wanting to reach for him, pull him into her life.

She had seen him only once before, thousands of miles away in a foreign country. She had never expected to meet him again. All right, so he thought he recognized her, but she had not admitted to knowing him, and he would be gone by now. On to the next country, wherever he had chosen to focus his lens this time.

Heaven help her if his latest book was a photo study of Canada!

She shook her head, her fingers curling tightly around the steering wheel. He had always photographed Third World countries, exotic places, and recently glimpses from the other side of the crumbled Iron Curtain. Not one of his books had focused on the Western world of civilization and uniformity. She had no idea what could have brought him to Victoria last weekend, but by now he must be long gone.

She put the van in motion again and drove along the twisting waterfront. The summer tourists were gone. The fleet of sailboats had faded, leaving the seashore for the permanent residents. Abby turned off onto the gravel side road, following the shape of the familiar drive, watching the trees and the scraps of wispy white scattered high in the blue sky. Just outside her own drive, she glanced back and saw the cloud of dust she had sent up. Driving too fast. She had to stop that, slow down, or old Mr. Walker would be knocking on her door again, complaining that the dust she made was coating his roses.

She passed her own drive and pulled into the next one, stopping in front of a ranch-style house. As she rolled down her window, her neighbor Sandra waved from the veranda.

"Hi! I'm back!" Abby announced. "I'm headed for a hot bath, then we're on for supper."

"Thank goodness!" said her neighbor with a grin. "If you see that cat of yours..." Sandra was thirty, a short brunette with a curvy, voluptuous body and runner's muscles. Today she was dressed in jeans and an oversize sweatshirt that demanded loudly, "Who needs men?" They had been friends for five years, ever since Abby and Trish moved into the house next door just as Sandra was in the middle of divorcing the man she insisted was the ogre to end all ogres.

"What's Tabby done now?" Abby asked warily.

"She's been catching mice again. Delivering them to my doorstep, since she can't find you."

Abby's lips twitched. "Sorry about that."

"Dead mice I can handle, but yesterday she brought a live one. She was playing with it and of course it got away, so now I have a mouse crunching through my walls at night." Sandra shrugged.

"Oh, dear..." Abby resisted laughter, but even Sandra's lips were twitching.

"I grew up on a farm. Mice are nothing. Just don't leave your window open nights or you'll wake up with a dead mouse on your bed. Or, heaven help you, a live one. Oh, and there was a very classy car down your drive on Monday."

"My mother." Ever since her widowed mother had married Damian Rule, she had been driving the Mercedes her husband gave her as a wedding present.

Sandra shrugged expressive shoulders. "I don't know. Didn't see it clearly. Drove in and back out again a few minutes later."

"She probably left me a note. Are we on for dinner tonight?"

"Your place or mine?"

"Mine. My fisherman in Campbell River gave me another salmon. I'll put it on the barbecue."

Tabby was waiting on the front porch when Abby drove into her own drive. She put the van in the garage and took the removable cartridge from her computer. She always did that first, taking it into her office and reading the data into her desktop computer. Then, with her client's data backed up, she was free to forget book-keeping.

She brought the cooler in next, with the salmon inside. She often came back with odds and ends, gifts from her clients. Fish from the fisherman who was happy that she could come to his boat to do the books. Fresh produce from the farmer just north of nearby Duncan.

She checked the fridge for a note from her mother, frowned when she found nothing. She went to her answering machine, turned it on and let it play while she walked into her bedroom to shed her shoes and panty hose.

"...Abby, it's Hans. I'll be down a week Saturday to see Patricia. I'd like to see her work as well..."

Good luck, she thought uneasily, wondering if she could put Hans off again. Difficult, when he had given her over a week's warning. She would have to talk to Trish about it this weekend. Tomorrow, when she picked her up from school...or perhaps it would be better to wait for Sunday afternoon. If Trish reacted badly, the silent rebellion could ruin their whole weekend.

The next message was from a client, a restaurateur in Nanaimo. Then her mother. "...Abby? Wasn't that a marvelous man! I've always thought Ryan was such a romantic name, and did you notice? He couldn't keep his eyes off you. Damian and I can't make this weekend. A silly banker's thing in Vancouver. Tell Trish next weekend, and we'll take her out for pizza. See you, love..."

Abby's hands clenched into the softness of her nylons. Just his name on her mother's lips and Abby could feel herself winding up like an overtensioned spring. She gnawed on her lower lip and forced her attention to the rest of the messages. Business. The manager of a garage had lost his business checkbook and could she order another from the bank. A traveling dentist wanted to know if he could afford a new workstation and was the interest rate he had been offered a good deal. That was all. The machine switched off.

Bare-legged and barefoot, Abby went from her bedroom to Trish's room. Last weekend Trish had stayed with friends in Duncan, had gone to her extra lessons while Abby went to Victoria for the showing of Benedict's work. Abby wandered around the room now, touching Trish's stuffed toys, the pile of books on the bedside table. Standing there amid her daughter's tidy clutter, she could almost pretend Trish was sprawled in the next room reading a book, or coming in from outside with Tabby in her arms.

Abby shook off the feeling of loneliness and went to run her bath. Afterward, clean and scented, lethargic from the warm water, she changed into jeans and a sloppy sweatshirt. The shirt sported two eagles in flight across her breasts, and the words "Normal is for the birds" written out below. It was a gift from Sandra, who was addicted to slogans.

Abby was lighting the barbecue when she heard the door knocker. "Come on in!" she shouted. She heard Sandra open the door, called out, "I'm out back, just lighting the coals to roast this fish. It's a beauty." She poured another stream of starter fluid on the coals, then struck the sparker and instinctively jerked back as the flames curled around the charcoal. Her hand reached to trap her hair, protect it from the flame, but the long strands were still caught back in the twist at the base of her neck.

Behind her, a voice spoke, making her blood pulse.

"Hello again," he said quietly.

She froze, then slowly turned to face him. He was standing in the kitchen doorway. "You look different," he said, his eyes taking in everything from her bare feet to her imprisoned hair. He was wearing jeans and sneakers today, and a chunky dark sweatshirt that only emphasized the breadth of his shoulders.

"Different?" she croaked. She swallowed, trying to clear her throat, and heard the sound she made, knowing he heard, too. Her hand went to the twist of hair at the back of her neck. She should have worn her hair up last weekend at the gallery. And her glasses, she thought, pushing the frames up with the back of her hand. He might not have recognized her if she had worn the glasses.

He stepped out onto the patio. She stepped back, away from him. The barbecue was between them, heating. "What do you want?" she whispered.

His head jerked, throwing an unruly streak of dark hair back from his forehead. She moved back again.

"Watch it or you'll fall off the edge!"

She stopped abruptly. He stopped coming closer then and she felt herself breathe again. She saw him looking at everything, one swift glance. The lawn chairs. The table that she and Trish used for summer meals outside. The swing set, hardly used because Trish said she was too old.

"Why are you here?"

"Unfinished business." He pushed a hand into his pocket. She realized then what was missing. The camera. In London, even at the showing, he'd had a camera. And that afternoon...

"Unfinished? I don't know what you're talking about." She jerked into motion, moving toward the house, away from him.

She knew he followed her into the kitchen, but she tried to ignore him and concentrate on the big Chinook salmon. She opened a cupboard door and took out foil to wrap the salmon.

He was there, leaning against the doorjamb. Any other man would seem idle, leaning against pillars and doors, watching. He didn't. He looked... dangerous. Ready to spring.

He said, "I saw it in your eyes."

She opened the fridge and got out an onion and some butter, felt her fingers clenched hard around the onion as he demanded softly, "Aren't you going to ask what I saw in your eyes?"

"No." She moved the fish to the chopping board with a slapping sound. She pulled a knife from a wooden block and began to chop the onion with surprisingly steady strokes.

"Memories," he said softly. "I saw memories."

She pulled the last of the peel away and sliced the onion in half. There was something fluttering deep inside her stomach, but her hands were steady.

"Memories," he repeated. "The same ones that have been in my dreams for eleven and a half years."

She laid slices of onion into the cavity of the salmon. "I don't know what you're talking about." She turned to face him, still holding the knife. "I don't want to know."

His gaze dropped to the knife, back to her face. "Are you thinking of attacking me with that?" he asked curiously, and she thought his lips twitched.

"I want you to leave. Go. Don't come back." Part of her knew that her words were lies, but she could not afford to let this man close. The onion fumes were crawling around her glasses, penetrating her eyes and making them tear. She moved to the sink, turned on the water, rinsed her hands and the knife, but it was too late to stop the tearing. "I didn't invite you here."

"When did you marry him?"

She dropped the knife into the sink and concentrated on the details of preparing the fish. Butter on the skin. Butter inside the cavity. A layer of onions in there, and onions lying on the skin. Salt and pepper, then she could wrap it with foil. She turned, the silver-wrapped fish in her hands, but he was standing there in her path.

He said harshly, "After what happened between you and me that afternoon...I could no more have gone to another woman than I could have taken my own life."

"Nothing happened. Nothing." She gulped.

He moved a step closer and her body went rigid with tension. He said softly, "Abigail... Your mother told me you were christened Abigail, but you've always been called Abby. Not Gail."

"I had an aunt named Gail. People confused our names."

"That afternoon, you told me Gail."

She shook her head. "Someone else. Not me." She knew denial was useless, but what else could she do? She stepped back as he moved, but the counter came up behind her and he was too close.

"It never happened," she whispered.

In London, his face had not been so harsh, the lines not so deeply engraved. She stared at him with wide, vulnerable eyes. Then, abruptly, he stepped back and she stumbled past him onto the patio deck.

She laid the foil-wrapped package on the barbecue grill and said, "I want you out of here. Now. Or I'll call the police."

"Who's sharing the salmon?"

"A friend."

"A man?"

She swallowed, wanted to lie, but said nothing.

"There's surely enough for three."

"Get out!" She heard the anger in her own voice, surprised because she had told herself that she felt only numbness. "Get out of my life!"

He rammed both hands into the back pockets of his jeans. She jerked back at the violence of the motion, but his voice came flat and hard. "Not until you tell me why you didn't meet me that Sunday in London. And how you could go from me to Benedict Stakeman."

She gripped her fingers together to stop the trembling. "You're an arrogant—do you think if a woman... that she'd never be able to be with another man without you in her... in her...?'' Burned into her soul. Her breath backed up in her chest, lungs aching with fire.

His hand caught her face again, fingers spread out to the curve of her cheek. She saw strength in his face, and determination. Somehow, he would take the truth from her and in doing so, he could destroy everything. She saw his jaw jerk with tension, felt his fingers curl into her
jaw.

"My name's not Gail," she whispered.

"For me it is," he replied harshly.

From the house, the sound of knocking echoed. Abby sagged with relief. "It's Sandra. She's come for dinner."

Sandra's voice rang out. "Hey, Abby? You in there?"

"Let me go," she whispered.

"Why should I?" His gaze swept her face. Her tongue darted out to wet nervous lips. She could feel the trembling deep inside her body.

"Aha! There you are, Abby! Who belongs to that gorgeous Porsche outside? You—— Oh!" Sandra's footsteps sounded, then her sandals clattered on the patio briefly.

Abby could not look away from his face. He was older. The same, but different. He had gained a hardness that made her nervous, uncertain what he might do. The harsh lines cut deeply on either side of his mouth. His brows were gathered together, frowning at her over a gaze gone opaque and dangerous. Abby's hands curled around his wrists, tried to push his hands away, free herself. Her fingers found the thick, dark hair that grew on the back of his forearm and she jerked back from the texture, but the feel of him echoed in her memory.

He let her go free.

Sandra was standing motionless, her lips parted on a gasp of surprise. Abby licked her lips, realizing that while this man's hand had been touching her she had forgotten Sandra's presence. Sandra was watching them.

"Sandra——"

Abby pushed her glasses into place, felt her breasts rise and fall in rapid panic. Get him out of here. Somehow, she must make him go away. He was watching her. He must know that her whole body was weak from his touch.

Sandra assessed Ryan speculatively. "We can have dinner another night."

"Good idea," said Ryan bluntly, and Sandra laughed.

Abby moved, getting farther away from him, closer to Sandra, who said, "You're a dark horse, Abby. Call me tomorrow and——"

"No! Stay! This is—he's just going!"

"Ryan," he said, his arm falling across Abby's shoulder, his fingers cupping her upper arm, his touch scalding her. "My name's Ryan." He looked down at Abby. She knew it was deliberate, intended to tell Sandra that they were more than friends.

Lovers.

"No," Abby whispered.

Abby saw his gaze move from her to Sandra and back again. Then he turned, moving slowly, and she was pinned motionless as if in a spider's web. It was some terrible game he was playing with her.

"I'll go," he said in a low voice. "But I'll be back. Meanwhile..."

She tried to say something.

He reached up and took her glasses away so that the harsh lines of his face were softened in her vision. Then he moved very close, his features coming clear and sharp again.

"I like the glasses," he whispered against her cheek. "I remember you without them, but I like your eyes this way. Framed. Wide and staring...the glasses...something for a man to take off...slowly."

He was going to kiss her. She tried to press her lips tightly. She knew she should pull away, but she could feel the heat radiating from his body and somehow she knew, as she had known that day so long ago, that this was written somewhere in ink and forever...that it would happen with or without her will.

There was anger in his eyes, but his mouth was gentle on hers. A tender kiss. She tried to be frozen, but her pulse beat hard and heavy. She jerked when his hand slid across her back, then she was close, his chest against her breasts, the pressure making them swell with the feel of him. His mouth moved to the vulnerable pulse at her throat and her head moved back, giving him access. She tried to stop the languid downward journey of her eyelids. Failed.

"Remember," he murmured almost inaudibly, his mouth returning to her mouth. "Do you remember this?"

Forever, her heart thundering, breath stopped.

Then he drew back.

He waited until her eyes opened before he said, "I knew you hadn't forgotten, Gail."

She tried to shake her head.

"I'll be back."

"No," she managed unsteadily.

"Yes." His fingers grazed her chin, then he carefully replaced her glasses. "Unlike you, I keep my promises."

He turned and walked away. She would have known his walk in the middle of any crowd. Twenty years from now, she would still know him. She knew so little of him, but every detail was burned indelibly onto her mind. Always there. Hidden. Waiting.

Karma, she thought. Fate. He was gone now. He would be back.

"Whew," breathed Sandra.

Abby jerked and glared at her friend. Sandra fluffed her dark hair out and whispered significantly, "Are you sure you don't want me to disappear? You could run out and catch him, tell him——"

"No!" She heard the faint sound of a car door slamming. "Sandra——" She had forgotten everything except the man staring down at her, holding her, kissing her.

The car's motor roared, then Abby heard wheels on gravel. She licked her lips, swallowed and said, "He's gone. I—he'll be back."

Sandra's lips twitched. "Lock the doors and pull up the drawbridge. Send him over to me if you like. What about that fish?"

They ate their dinner out on the patio. Then, when Sandra was gone, Abby went to her office and worked until three in the morning, tidying up details she would normally have worked on the next day.

Eventually, she went to bed and tried to sleep, then gave up when the sun rose and called her mother on the telephone.

"Mom? That man you met at the showing...?"

"Nice, wasn't he?" She could hear the smile in her mother's voice. Abby closed her eyes.

"No, that's not it. I——" The trembling started in her hands again.

Sarah said, "He was interested in you. Anyone could tell that. And you——"

"Mom! I——" Abby gripped the receiver more tightly. "I got a call from someone who wants to get in touch with—with—he's some kind of photographer, isn't he?" Abby's gaze went to the bookcase where she knew his first book lay nestled between an atlas and a pictorial history of the world. "He's not Canadian, is he? So I imagine he's gone now, back to wherever——"

"British," said her mother. "But educated in France and the States. His parents were diplomats, you know."

She did not want to know.

"...back from three years in South America," her mother was saying. So there would be a book on South America next, thought Abby. "Next assignment. Flying to New York on Monday. But, Abby, if your friend wanted Ryan to take photos—that's not the sort of thing he does. He used to be a news photographer, years back, but he's famous now for these books he does. Portraits of the soul of a country, the bookstore clerk told me. The clerk also said that Ryan's first book has just gone into its fifth printing, and—so he's not likely to be interested in ordinary photo commissions. You'd better tell your friend to find an ordinary photographer."

On Monday he would be gone to New York. She would never see him again. She felt a sickness in her stomach that she told herself was relief.

"Look, Abby, I'll call him. He's staying at the Royal Oak. I'll ask him to call you back, shall I?"

"No! Mom, *don't* do that!"

"Say my name," he had insisted, years ago, his fingers burning her cheek.

Her mother was trying to tell her more about the handsome stranger. Abby squeezed her eyes closed, tried not to hear, asked desperately, "I—how was your week? And what's this thing coming off in Vancouver? You said you couldn't make it this weekend."

As a device to deflect her mother to another topic, it did not work. Sarah said, "We had Ryan to dinner Wednesday night. Damian quite liked him, which isn't usual, you know. Damian's got this thing about artists. Although, I suppose photography is different."

Her stepfather had quiet, decided opinions on a lot of things. Abby had had a few arguments with him about Trish's schooling, but the important thing was that her mother was happy again after years of lonely widowhood.

Abby said, "About next weekend, Mom. Hans will be there."

"Oh-oh!" Her mother drew in a sharp breath. "Hans and Damian will clash, don't you think?"

"Yes." Abby smothered a laugh. "Although I'm sure Damian will enjoy a good argument, and having him here might deflect Hans. He's coming to look at Trish's work, and you know how productive she *hasn't* been! And...well, you know Hans."

Sarah sighed and decided, "All right, we'll come. Shall I tell Damian to feel free to take on Hans?"

"Don't you dare. It'll be fireworks around here anyway, without encouraging him."

Electricity, Sandra had said. You could see the electricity. Sparks, when all he had done was touch her face with his hand, caress her shoulder and her back, bend his lips to her mouth and find the gasp at her throat.

"What will you do this weekend?" her mother asked.

Vancouver. She would take Trish to Vancouver. They would stay in that hotel on English Bay, prowl the beach and maybe do some shopping. She was not about to confide her plans in her mother, not now. Just how friendly was her mother with Ryan Marsdon? Dinner on Wednesday, and she knew which hotel in Victoria he'd chosen to stay in. He must have pumped Sarah Rule so skillfully that she'd not even known he was coming here to confront Abby. To ask her why she had married

Benedict Stakeman, why she had failed to keep a date
with Ryan Marsdon over eleven years ago.

Abby remembered giving that promise. She would have
said anything to get away from him that day in London.

CHAPTER THREE

MEMORIES came to her in the darkest hours, when the moon was gone and starlight masked by clouds. She opened her eyes and saw only shadows on shadows. And yesterday.

For her twenty-first birthday her mother had given her tuition at any night school course she chose to take. Abby signed up for a course in oil painting at the community college; evening relaxation after days as a bookkeeper.

She remembered that first evening; the tall, distinguished man with the dreamer's eyes—an artist who had stepped down to share his knowledge with a night class of amateurs. Benedict Stakeman.

She had no sense of color, he told her kindly, but he could teach her enough that she could enjoy doodling. She knew that his paintings were being shown in galleries both in Victoria and overseas in London. If he could teach her, she would be happy to learn. She was aware, with breathless excitement, that all through the class he watched her.

After the second class, he took her out for coffee and persuaded her to drop the course. "I'd like to see you," he said in a voice that made her uncertain just what he wanted. "But let's not mix painting into it. If you're determined, take a course from someone else. You'll never be an artist, but there's no reason you can't play around and have fun."

He wanted her to understand about his art, he said. Then he watched her intently, his eyes memorizing each feature as he asked her in a quiet, intense voice whether she dreamed of having children, a family. She dressed like a bookkeeper or a schoolgirl, he said. He taught her to dress, to grow a smooth mask for the showings he took her to. With her fair hair and her white flesh, with those wide innocent eyes, he told her that she would cast a spell on the world of art. The glasses, of course, would have to go.

It was a game he taught her to play, although he became angry when she called it a game. He never painted her. Under that superficial mystery of eyes and skin, she had the wrong bone structure. Instead, he had her painted by Hans Bunian before they were married.

She was breathless, caught in a dream come true. The mad whirl of leaving her bookkeeping job, giving up her apartment, storing things at her mother's because Ben said, "Leave it all, it doesn't fit you."

The wedding, walking up the aisle on her uncle's arm, seeing Ben waiting for her, tall and distinguished, oddly overshadowed by Hans Bunian's heavy, muscular form. Hans was best man, his gray hair tamed for the occasion, and Abby was nervous of his heavy gruffness.

Abby's mother, smiling with tears in her eyes, remembering her own marriage to the man she had loved until his death only a year before.

Ben took her to Malibu, California, where he had rented a beach house for the honeymoon that went on for months. They would have a son, he told her, his eyes narrowed and dreamy. With Abby's facile talent for sketching and Ben's own great talent, their son would be a great artist—following in his father's footsteps.

"He'll look like me," Ben told her one night as they stood on the veranda looking out over the dark water. He turned her face so that he could study her in the moonlight. "I have all the dominant traits. Your blue

eyes and fair hair won't have a chance. He'll be *my* son."
It was the first shadow, that night. She had stared back
at him as a sick conviction grew that he had chosen her
for her lack of dominant characteristics...her minor
talent for drawing.

To give Benedict Stakeman the son he craved.

Later, the panic faded and she knew that she had been
foolish to fear he did not love her, but she tried harder
to be the woman he wanted. She never quite succeeded.
She hated the contact lenses that made her eyes ache.
She had an unfortunate tendency to kick off her shoes
and walk barefoot on the beach just as people came to
the door. When guests came, Ben insisted that she play
her "great artist's wife" part, although she always felt
so stiff and awkward in that role.

At night, in their bedroom, she knew that she disappointed him.

When she gave him a son...

Each time she failed to conceive, his need for a child
grew.

"Is that why you married me?" she demanded once
in painful frustration. "To breed your descendants?
Don't you love me at all? Me?"

He glared at her with dark eyes turning wild, then he
threw his coffee cup across the kitchen so that it burst
into shattered pieces, the dark liquid exploding everywhere. He never answered her painful question. She
never asked again. Secretly, she went to a doctor, a kindly
man who laughed and told her to relax. Give it time.
She felt herself becoming nervous, losing the casual confidence that had once been hers. When she watched Ben
painting on the beach veranda, she wondered if each
seascape was only an echo of the last.

Time, the doctor said, and in the middle of a
California winter Abby believed that her prayers had

been answered. Her period was late. When she confided in Ben, he took her out dancing and told her he loved her.

It was the first time he had actually said the words. "I love you."

He left her the next morning. He flew to Toronto, then to Mexico City, calling her each night, asking after his son always. She prayed it would be a boy.

"Have you been to the doctor yet?" he asked one night, his voice distorted by the Mexican telephone system.

She felt the hopeless sense of failure welling up. That day her woman's body had failed her. She did not know how to say the words to him. Not on the telephone.

"Yes," she whispered, and somehow the lies grew from there.

Impossible to tell him on the telephone. She would tell him the truth, of course. Later, when they were together, when she could touch his hand and . . . tell him she had learned from the doctor how to measure her own time of fertility. They would try again.

Early in March, he called in the small hours of the night. She had reached out for the telephone, only half awake when his voice came in her ear.

"Come to London," he demanded in a buoyant voice. "I want you in London. Fly."

"All right," she agreed, wiping the sleep from her eyes. London, where she would have to find the words to tell him of her failure. "When?"

He gave her time and flight, said his agent would arrange her ticket. "Pack everything and send it back to Victoria. We're done with Malibu."

"I—— Yes. All right."

"I'm having a showing in London, starting Friday. So I'll see you in London! Take care of my son!"

"A showing? But—you didn't tell me."

She heard his laughter and, behind it, the sound of one of those all-night artists' parties. She trembled, thinking that perhaps it was wrong to tell him. With her new knowledge of her own cycle, perhaps she could...make the lie into truth.

He met her at the airport, a big man with dark hair and excited brown eyes. She had put in her contact lenses in the washroom of the big jet, had freed her hair and brushed it down around her shoulders the way he liked it.

He caught her in his arms as she came through the Customs check, swinging her, laughing and whispering in a loud voice, "I'll have to be gentle, won't I, darling?" He dropped a significant glance to her flat abdomen. A woman nearby smiled with amused tolerance.

"Ben——"

"Come on. They're waiting!"

She wanted to tell him in the limousine, but, each time, she tried, he rode over her words with his own excitement.

"I'm a sensation," he told her with a grin. "You knew I would be, didn't you?" His eyes turned somber and critical as the taxi slowed. "Comb your hair, darling. It's mussed. And try not to blink like that."

She knew she should have tried harder to tell him, should have insisted, because as soon as they were in that crowd of hangers-on at the gallery he started telling people. "The mother of my son...no, not for a few months yet...you're the first to know. Come to the christening. We're going to call him Patrick Benedict. He'll be an artist, like his father."

Strange painted lips making kissing motions at her cheek. Congratulations and laughter. Abby tried to pull

Ben aside to some quiet place where she could tell him; knew that she could never tell him...that she must.

They left the gallery with a crowd of people she had never seen before. The woman with the long cigarette holder kept puffing smoke into Abby's face, turning her pasted smile to a mask for nausea. When the taxi came, the strangers faded away, to Abby's relief. She was weary beyond measure. Jet lag, she thought. And fear, because he would be so upset. Especially now, after he had told the world.

He did not love her, she realized miserably as she sat beside him in that taxi. He wanted her to fit his image of a wife and mother, as if she were a painting he could twist to his will with a sable brush and colors. She closed her eyes and admitted painfully to herself that she had married a dream, a painter she admired. She had called it love, but this was real and her life might never come right.

"I'm not ready for sleep yet," he told her with a laugh. "Let's go dancing!"

He was always a creature of moods. He locked himself away when the painting fever was on him; burned midnight oil when he came out to play after weeks of solitude. She went with him to one club after another, a smile pasted stiffly on her face. The smoky bars made her nauseous, while the press of social bodies seemed almost claustrophobic. When they left the last nightclub, she put her head back against the taxi seat and closed her eyes, his voice washing over her, his burning energy that she found so exhausting. Jet lag, she told herself. Jet lag and tension from that horrible scene at the showing, Ben telling everyone in the world about the child she would have.

She would tell him tomorrow, when he was down from this manic high mood. I'm not pregnant after all. The words echoed again and again in her mind, and she drifted until she failed even to murmur agreement when his voice stopped.

When the collision came, she hardly knew what had happened.

She must have been sleeping, her head on her husband's shoulder. She'd not been belted in, she knew that. When she opened her eyes, she was staring up at pale blue eyes in a worried young face.

"Here! She's coming around!" a man in white shouted.

Hands lifting her. Distorted faces. Uniforms. Confusion everywhere.

"What happened?" she'd whispered.

No one answered.

"Where's Ben?" she demanded weakly.

It seemed hours before anyone answered her questions. The hospital. Emergency ward, she supposed. "I'm fine," she insisted, hearing her own voice echoing strangely in her ears. "Where is my husband? Is he all right?"

It was hours before she got away from the tendrils of the emergency room. A young intern just going off duty took her somewhere in an elevator, sat her down in a chair in a bleak waiting room with pastel walls.

"Stay here," he instructed her. "The surgeon will come to see you when your husband is out of OR."

No one would tell her anything. Incredibly, she must have slept, her head fallen back against the wall behind the chair. A nurse brought her tea and she drank it, telling herself it was proof that she'd crossed the world, because in America coffee was the cure-all. She sipped the tea, her eyes burning because she had slept with her contact lenses in. They were soft contacts, advertised as easy to wear. Abby suspected that her body would never grow to tolerate them.

She woke abruptly, jerking upright and staring at a man dressed in operating room clothes.

He said, "I'm sorry."

"Ben——"

"We couldn't save him." His voice droned on in perpetual monotone. Details she could not seem to absorb. She was supposed to do something tomorrow. Contact someone. The words washed over her endlessly.

"The nurse will call a taxi to take you home."

She wasn't sure just where home was. North America somewhere. Her possessions and Ben's were somewhere between Malibu and Victoria. His plans for their future were a mystery to her.

How could he be gone?

Then she was at the hotel, paying for the taxi with American dollars because she had no British money, watching the doorman moving toward her and trying to remember how she had come to be here.

Inside, she said her name, her voice hollow. The desk clerk gestured for someone to show her to the room. He said something about her husband. She heard but could not answer, could not tell him Ben was dead. She walked behind the uniformed porter and kept putting one foot in front of the other until she was inside the lush suite Ben had taken.

She closed the door in the porter's face, then realized that he had expected a tip. She shrugged. It did not matter. Nothing mattered. Her suitcase was lying on the luggage rack in the big double bedroom. It looked strange there, out of place.

Flowers on the bureau.

Numbly, she took the card from the bouquet.

"For the mother of my child. Ben."

She took out her contact lenses and lay on the bed, eyes wide-open to the light coming in through the curtains. It was tomorrow already, and she could not make her eyes close. Ben. It should hurt, but she felt only numbness. Seconds ticked past in her head, minutes, until she stood up abruptly, aware of her rumpled skirt, aware that she was in a strange country. She had no money to speak of. Ben had always looked after the money. The hotel bill...

She tried to worry about the hotel bill, but it did not seem to matter. She had no British money, only Ben's credit cards and a few American dollars. She thought the credit cards would be void now. She tried to care, to think about it. Anything to make her feel alive. She went numbly into the shower and stood in pounding cold water for a long time, then she dressed carefully, choosing the blue shirtwaister dress because Ben said she looked pretty in blue and she owed him that. No, he had not exactly said pretty. He'd said...

She put the lenses back in. Ben did not like her in glasses. Then she left the room, carrying her handbag and nothing else, taking the elevator down and walking through the lobby as if she were going somewhere. Someone called her name quietly as she crossed the lobby, but she kept walking. One foot in front of the other.

Outside.

She wondered if it was morning or afternoon. The drizzle that penetrated London made it seem more like darkness than light, but there was sun somewhere. She wondered what the shadows were doing, because Ben always worried about shadows. She walked past the doorman, keeping her eyes averted because she could not make her lips smile. She felt stiff, cast in plastic like a doll moving through the rain.

The gallery was near the hotel. Somehow, her feet took her there. Two blocks down and one over, Ben had said, and she hardly felt her feet moving on the pavement. She knew that she was getting wet, felt the weight of her long hair as it took up drops of rain. Had she forgotten to dry it properly when she showered? She tipped her head back and looked up. Drops of rain fell into her eyes, soothing the burning sensation from the lenses.

Had Ben died because she'd failed him? The world spun slowly and she jerked her head down, looking ahead, moving steadily until she recognized the entrance to the gallery. She went up the steps, almost floating. Sensations played along her back. Proof she was alive, she told herself. Proof she was not plastic. She moved her lips and felt their stiffness.

She had to see the paintings. Ben's paintings. She would walk along the aisles formed by artificial walls bearing paintings in oil. He always painted in oil, said it was more real. *She* had no sense of color. He had said that, and she knew it was true. That was why she sometimes looked at one of his paintings and thought it was only a copy of his other work. Today she would look and she would see the truth, the answer.

She walked halfway across the wide marble foyer before she stopped. Marble stairs led upward to another exhibit. Downstairs, a wide expanse drew viewers toward the featured exhibit.

Benedict Stakeman's paintings in oil.

There was a woman standing just inside the doorway to the Stakeman exhibit. That long cigarette holder. Abby recognized the line of movement as the woman waved her arm. She felt disoriented. She had come here expecting—crazily—to find the gallery empty, to move quietly and alone along the aisles, looking at Ben's

paintings. Not people. All those people, watching her.
Talking to her. Asking...asking...

She turned abruptly. Up the marble stairs. She was
aware of walking through a dream. The people were
strange, artificial...plastic. She floated up, came to rest
for a moment staring at a picture of a man with a camera.

Not paintings, up here. Flashes of shocking reality.
Photographs, blown up to tear away the viewer's image
of a gentle world. Abby walked slowly past the man's
picture, through his works, those giant photographs on
either side. Glimpses of places that came on the news,
harsh life and death to tear off blinders forever. She had
the illusion that she was moving across a mine field, feet
placed carefully to navigate a safe course between these
hazards.

She saw him leaning against a pillar at the edge of the
crowd. Someone was talking to him, but he was not
listening. He should have been a harsh man, merciless,
but when his gaze took hold of hers she saw the man
behind it all and she knew him. She could see it all in
his eyes. Tenderness and caring and loving.

He came to her slowly, steadily, moving through the
watchers, the people who had come to pay homage to
his images. When he was staring down at her, she said,
"Do you ever see love through that lens?"

Her fingers brushed the camera hanging at his side.
His gaze did not follow her gesture, but stayed locked
on hers. "I see you," he said in an odd voice. "I'm
Ryan. Who are you?"

"Ryan," she repeated, and the name echoed somewhere. "What do you see?"

His fingers brushed her throat and were gone. She felt
a strange tingling crawling along her flesh, down across
her breasts to her midriff. Cold. The dampness from

outside settling into her bones now. He said quietly, "I want to take your picture."

He was tall and dark and impenetrable, but she could see through the mask. Because she was plastic, not real, she could see through the hard man to something strong and tender beneath.

She heard her own voice as a stranger's, telling him, "There's another showing downstairs."

"Yes," he agreed. "Take your choice. Reality, or fantasy."

His vision was harsher than reality, while Ben's...

"You look like him," she said, and it was true in a superficial way. Height, strong face, dark eyes that were brown only at first glance. If she narrowed her eyes and let things slip away a little...

He said with amusement, "We're worlds apart, I assure you. Will you let me photograph you?"

"You're British?" She realized she was clinging to words, conversation.

"More or less." He took her arm and she felt dizziness welling up, wondered if she would faint. Jet lag, she thought. It must be jet lag.

"Too many people," she said faintly.

For a moment, as he touched her arm, she knew that he was real, stark against all the shadows around her. He moved and she was following, going where he led. Stairs somewhere. Not the massive marble, but private, narrower.

"The back way," he murmured, "I've been desperate to get out of that place for hours." He stopped halfway down the stairs, brushing her hair back from her face and said huskily, "You're an angel sent to free me. More real than any of them."

"Not real," she whispered, shaking her head and feeling the damp tendrils of her hair clinging to her cheek. "I'm a ghost."

They slipped out into the rain and when he turned her to face him, there was warmth in his eyes. She wondered what he saw in hers.

"Magic," he whispered. "Your eyes. I can see myself in them, and I'm a stranger." He brushed a thumb along the curling edges of her lashes and asked in a soft, harsh voice, "Who the hell are you?"

A dream. "Are you going to take my picture?" she asked, wondering if the film could record a ghost.

"Oh, yes."

She could see faint threads of silver buried in the black of his rain-glistened hair. She said somberly, "Ghosts don't leave an image on film."

"You're no ghost." He curled his fingers through hers and for a few moments she lost track. Then he was opening a door. She walked past him. She remembered the porter then, and she had forgotten to tip him. She turned and frowned, because this was not her hotel room at all. The porter... then she saw the pictures on the wall and forgot everything. She walked slowly past each one. A long room, pictures and the sofa and a corner that was a kitchen, a bed far off in the corner.

He was standing in the doorway. As she watched, he pushed the door closed. Why had she come? Did he expect that she would go to that bed with him and...?

The camera was there, slung over his shoulder, hanging tucked behind his hip as if it were more familiar than his closest friend. She was surrounded by reality, all those prints, stark life screaming anger to the world outside.

"Why don't you show the love?" she asked quietly. Pain everywhere. Prints drying on a rack against one wall. A door half-open to a darkroom. Images blown up on the walls. She whispered, "How can you live here with their eyes watching you?"

"I change them." He moved slowly toward the wall where a scene of war invaded the room. She stared at it and could not feel it, knew it was the numbness crawling through her veins. Ben, she thought, but his name echoed hollow.

He said, "I take them down, put others up."

His words echoed through her mind as if she could see the letters painted there. Take them down. Put others up. She moved past him, touched the image of a woman's shoulder. She heard herself saying in a wistful voice, "She loves someone. There must be love and hope in her life, or she would have given up by now. Don't you see it?"

He turned to stare at the huddled image of a woman sheltering near a fire. "Why would she hope?"

Abby frowned. If he saw life and hope, might it change what was inside her? She whispered, "Because she's real. She's alive, and she's a mother."

She watched his eyes, brown and gold and green all mixed up, probing where there was nothing but numbness to probe. She said, "Women know life is more than war and killing," not knowing if it was true any more. She touched his arm, felt warmth and caring there and said quietly, "Men have to learn it, but women are born knowing."

It was forever, their eyes together passing messages she could not quite hear. Then he took her hands and led her to the gray light from the window. He did not live in this room, she thought. Not really. He lived out there, with a camera in front of his eyes. This place was only a stop between journeys.

"Tell me your name," he demanded, his long fingers curled around her hands.

"Gail," she said, because she was not real and she had never been Gail.

"Say my name," he demanded.

His name. Ryan. She tried to let it fade from her consciousness. A name would make him real...nothing was real.

"Say it," he demanded in a low voice that knew its own power. "Ryan...say it. You said it at the gallery. Say it again."

She shook her head. She saw the lens cap going off his camera, watched him with wide eyes as he snapped one picture, then another. Then he touched her chin and stared down into her eyes. "Take those lenses out of your eyes," he ordered. "Over there."

She went into the room, closed the door and saw her own face in the mirror. She was blinking too often, her eyes protesting as they always did. She fumbled in her purse for the lens case and took the contact lenses out, but she did not put her glasses on.

Everything was softer around the edges when she went back to him. She heard the camera before she saw it, a man snapping images of a ghost who could see only shapes and colors, no edges, no lines. She thought the softness would mute the pain that was beginning to penetrate the numbness, but somehow it could not. She saw his face emerging from the soft blur of her vision. When she was close enough to see his eyes, she sank down on the long sofa that he must have bought specially to take his long form.

She wanted to ask him to hold her, because she was ice and cold and lonely and frightened. He sat beside her, touching her face and looking into her eyes. "That's better," he whispered, and even without clear vision she saw too much in his eyes. His hand touched her cheek and she felt it. She knew that she must not feel. She must be only a ghost, slipping through a dream.

Ben . . .

She closed her eyes and reached for Ben's face. He touched her lips with his, Ben's kiss on her mouth.

"Say my name," he whispered.

Lies, she thought. Lies, night after night on the telephone. Somehow, he had known and she'd killed him with her lies.

"I have to go." She recognized her own voice, told herself she should move, turn the words into action. She felt so tired. Weary down beneath her bones.

The man with a camera raised it. "Shh," he whispered. "Just stare at me, watch me." She heard the click. Again and again, the sound of the camera. He brushed her hair back behind her shoulder, said tensely, "Just undo three buttons, let the collar fall across your shoulder."

His face, showing behind the black body of the camera he thought would capture her image. He did not realize there would be no image, nothing on the film when it came out of the developing solution.

His lips came close and he brushed hers with them. "Say my name," he whispered. She touched her own lips with her fingers, felt the echo of his mouth on hers. Strange, she thought. Sensation. A dream, but dreams left only shadows when they faded. The grayness from outside bathed his studio in a dim light that was part of the fantasy. He touched her lips with his fingers. He had long fingers, callused. Hard skin, gentle on her face.

Abruptly, he was *too* real. She tried to reach for Ben but his memory slipped away. She gasped, pain floating close, then gone.

"Say my name," he demanded. His lips almost touched hers as he spoke. "Ryan . . . say it, Gail."

He took her lips with rough softness. Could he take the numbness away? "Ryan," he whispered hypnotically.

"Ryan," she echoed weakly.

Hands touching, forming, seeing the shape of her. A voice hoarse with feeling, fingers so gentle. She found her eyes closed and thought the tears would come, but there were no tears. She opened her eyes again and found his gaze turned dark with emotion.

"Do you believe in fate?" he asked harshly.

Severe, like the pictures on the wall, but she could see through the curtain as if it had never been there. "Yes," she whispered. "You are my fate."

She felt her own fingers on her throat, heard a shaken whisper from his throat as she released the buttons of her bodice slowly, one by one. His touch was warm, so warm. Inside, she was so cold.

Touching... arms holding her close... drifting... dreaming... warmth. Someone cried out, and she knew somewhere that it was her own voice on the still air of a London afternoon.

Then nothing, only the darkness of deep sleep. Exhaustion. Peace.

Hours later, she came to consciousness slowly, heavy from long sleep. She remembered arms holding her, her own tears inside. She opened her eyes and saw an uncurtained window, a hazy brick wall and the gray sky.

His voice said, "I thought you'd sleep forever."

He was standing at the side of the bed, wearing a battered pair of jeans, looking down at her with just a hint of a smile that seemed impossibly clear to her hazy vision. It would have been a confused dream lying in her waking consciousness, except that he was here, holding out a steaming mug and saying, "You've slept for hours, you know. Coffee?"

She took it and curled her fingers around the warmth of the mug, stared into the steam and could think of nothing to say. Everything was clear to her, the showing and the hospital and Ben who would never paint again. But reality was here and now, sitting in a bed with nothing covering her but a sheet, pictures of destruction on the walls all around. Reality was sitting motionless, gripping a warm cup of coffee while a stranger with warm eyes gently brushed a confusion of hair out of her eyes.

He said in a husky voice, "I have to go out," and she heard regret in his voice. "But I'll be back soon."

She made some motion with her shoulders. As if it were words, he understood and said, "No. Stay here. I won't be long."

She watched the steam rising from the cup. She had slept, had drowned in darkness while his arms held her. Those arms. Now they were propped on his knees as he leaned toward her. She watched the steam rising from her coffee, but her eyes saw his denim-covered thighs and knees. Saw his arms, hands moving slightly as he talked.

"I can't," she said. "I can't stay." So strange that her voice was clear.

How could she have lain here in this bed with . . . a stranger? Yesterday—was it yesterday that she had walked with him into this room? Yesterday that he had seemed a man she had known forever?

He was a stranger. An ax murderer, for all she knew. Certainly a man who took frightening pictures. Whatever had happened—it was shock, or jet lag—whatever excuse she tried to make, she had to get out of here. Fast.

"Why can't you stay?"

"I just can't."

He took the mug away and wrapped his fingers around hers. She felt the heat again and knew that whatever excuses she made to herself, she had no defences against this man. He said, "Meet me tomorrow, then. At the gallery. At twelve noon. I need to see you again." His thick eyebrows had lowered over his eyes. "Gail?"

She blinked and perhaps she nodded.

"You'll be there? Promise?"

"Yes," she agreed.

"Yesterday afternoon..." His voice faded, then he said softly, "Gail, I didn't take any precautions yesterday."

She understood his meaning and felt her flesh warming. "It doesn't matter," she said, pulling away.

"You're sure that nothing——?"

"Yes," she said abruptly. "I'm...sure." She had to leave, but she was trapped under the sheet. Naked under the sheet.

"The last thing I need is chains, but——" His voice was strained. "I almost..." He touched her hair and she heard his voice demanding, "Do you feel what I feel, Gail?"

She told herself that she felt nothing.

CHAPTER FOUR

ABBY heard the wheels on the drive outside.

She knew who it was.

Nemesis. Justice. Time...catching up with her.

She opened the door before the echo from the knocker had faded. Ryan was wearing a black bomber jacket open over a red cotton shirt and faded jeans. The strap of his camera showed across one shoulder. The camera itself, she knew, would be slung to hang lying in the hollow at the back of his waist.

His hair was sprawling over his forehead as if the breeze had freed it, dark and virile and flecked with silver. She held the door in one hand, her body a barricade across the doorway. Everything about him was quiet and dangerous. His mouth—not smiling, not frowning. His eyes could be hazel or brown or green, any color he needed. Now they were almost black.

Dangerous.

"My mother said you were going to New York on Monday."

"Yes." Nothing changed in his eyes, just a flicker of tension across his mouth. "But you knew I'd be back."

Yes, she had known.

"Are you going to let me in?" His gaze dropped to her bare feet and she resisted the urge to shift them nervously. She felt her fingers curl in and forced them to relax, not to rub the sudden dampness of her palms away on the denim of her jeans.

Behind him, the tall green trees in front of her house bent in the wind. She fought the image of his masculine form erect in the forest, wildness all around and civilization somewhere on the other side of the world. She stepped back just as Trish's streaky-colored cat twisted around their two sets of legs and stretched into the living room.

Inside, Tabby turned and silently challenged the invader, but even the cat knew he would come in if he wanted to. This was not a man you could stop with words. Abby knew she could probably send him away, but he would return until he was the one to decide there was no more need to come. He walked in, moving into the quiet shadow of her living room. She followed him.

Trish was away at school until tomorrow afternoon. Twenty-four hours. Was that time enough to send him away? He prowled across the living room, stared through her window to the trees that gave an illusion of country and wilderness.

"Do you want a cup of coffee?"

"Why not?" He smiled. "I like your place. Secluded. Nice."

"It's not all that secluded." There was no sign of her trembling pulse in her voice. She gestured toward the trees. "Sandra's house is through that way. You can't see it, but it's there."

"Sandra?" His voice was curious. "Your friend from last week?"

"Yes. She's...she works at the nightclub near the marina."

"You're good friends?"

"Yes." Sandra was her only close woman friend.

He pulled the zip of the bomber jacket the rest of the way down, giving it a jerk at the bottom so the two sides hung free. "How long have you been neighbors?" Under the jacket, his cotton shirt was tucked in over an abdomen that was still flat and hard, a waist that...

She tucked a strand of hair behind her ear, forced her gaze to his face. "Five years. I bought this place when..."

When Trish went to private school. She had wanted her daughter to come home each weekend to something warmer than a city apartment. Losing her during the week had made her feel frightened, guilty, although there seemed no choice.

"She's married?"

"Divorced," said Abby abruptly. She saw her sandals lying just inside the closed door he had come through only moments ago. She moved to them, slipped them on and felt crazily less vulnerable. She said, "If you want to ask Sandra out, I'd suggest you try the direct approach."

He laughed and she flushed angrily.

He said quietly, "I wondered how long the restraint would last. I remember you as painfully blunt, soft voice and penetrating words, although there was one hell of a lot you had hidden away back then."

Hidden. She was afraid he would pursue that. Every moment spent with him held mine fields for her, disaster waiting. If he ever found out...

She wasn't sure what he would do, did not want to know.

"Two women alone?" he speculated. "Neighbors? Side by side? Hiding from life?"

She snapped, "If you've come to make problems for me, I wish you'd go."

She watched him prowling on her carpet, from the window to the fireplace...back along the low bookshelves that lined her walls...towards the dining room...his brown fingers caressing the antique oak finish of the dining table she used only for company. She stared at the rhythmic stroking of his fingers on the warm oak, licked her lips and tried to think of something to say.

Her eyes focused on the cat and he asked, "How long have you had the cat?"

Ever since Trish brought it home from the beach last month. Her lips parted, closed, then she said uncomfortably, "She was a stray. She was...on the beach. She's not friendly."

He bent down, crooked his index finger and gently rubbed the cat's jaw. Tabby evaluated him for a long moment, then stretched her neck to lean into the caress.

"I waited for you," Ryan said, his eyes on the cat.

She swallowed, felt her heart crash against her ribs before it began to race breathlessly.

"At the gallery," he continued tonelessly. "That Sunday." He made a V of his fingers, stroking both sides of the cat's jaw at the same time. Tabby's purr shifted into high volume. "Where were you?"

His face was hard and lined by life, incongruous against the soft fur of the cat he was stroking. He shifted and Tabby was in his arms. He stroked her neck and the touchy cat curled there as if she were a cuddly sort of beast.

"Where were you?" His voice had turned harsh.

He said it had been a Sunday, although the days of the week had meant nothing to her. She had left that studio, had walked and walked and ended up back at the hotel. She remembered going in, through the entrance, the uniformed doorman ushering her through. Then *they* had taken over—the people who had surrounded Ben in life. Someone must have called Ben's agent, because he had flown over. Hans Bunian, too.

"Where were you? Why did you walk out of the hospital like that? We've been worried."

Hans, glowering at her, then his gray hair replaced by neutral brown. A doctor. There must have been some kind of sedative then, although she had been numb beyond comprehension. But she had slept.

She remembered, just as the doctor was about to slide the needle under her skin, Hans warning him that Abby was pregnant. Her lips had parted on a silent denial.

Again, Ryan asked, "Where were you while I was waiting for you at the gallery?" Although his voice had risen, Tabby curled more deeply into his arms.

"I was...in my hotel," she answered finally. "Or...on a jet. To Vancouver."

"Did you think of me?" Tabby protested and he let her free. He turned away to prowl along the wall, exploring the books in the cases. "Did you?"

"Yes," she whispered, although she had intended to deny it.

"But you left regardless?" He stopped and crouched down to look at the books. His fingers slid along the bindings. He touched everything. She tried not to remember. It was not real, had not *been* real. She tried to look away from his hands. He had been somewhere the sun beat hot and long. Even his fingers were darkened from the sun. Tabby stretched a paw up onto his knee as his touch stopped on the atlas.

He pulled out the book next to it, balanced it on his knee as he opened the cover and turned two pages. He asked softly, "Why did you buy it?"

"I don't know." She felt vaguely ill, wished she would faint and knew escape would never be that easy.

His fingers smoothed the almost empty page. "I was looking for you."

"I know you were." She knew the words on that page. The dedication of that first book of his. "For Gail, the ghost who walked away."

The cover snapped closed. He pushed the book back into the shelf with suppressed violence. "You changed everything. Did you know that?"

She shook her head in denial. She should move, go into the kitchen. Coffee. A beer for him, perhaps. Anything to turn this into the kind of conversation that did not matter. When he stood straight, he was closer than she had thought he would be. He murmured, "Life isn't all war and killing. Do you remember saying that?"

Her gaze, meeting his, denied the memory.

"For a year I couldn't take a picture that would turn out." He prowled along the edge of the room, looking out, touching the window frame. "I went to Iran. To Israel. I couldn't even see what was in front of me." His voice was alive with suppressed frustration. "I kept wondering what *your* eyes would see, and——" An angry sound exploded in his throat. "I started seeing the world through *your* eyes. The eyes you gave me."

"No!"

"I thought you were truth." His jaw tensed, making the words come out ragged and hard. "Who the hell were you?" He crossed the room and she tried to move out of his path, but his fingers touched her cheek, tracing along the curve in the parody of a touch from her dreams. "You told me you were a ghost."

"Don't," she whispered.

His eyes were alive with emotions, prying into hers as if they could find the depths that were hidden from everyone else. "Why did you marry him?"

In the dream, there had been tenderness and questions in his eyes. Now there was something almost like hatred. Resentment. "Just—please just go away," she whispered. "Go back wherever you——"

He ground out, "Why did you marry him after you were with me?"

After. As if he had no idea that Benedict Stakeman had died during that London exhibition. Surely he must have known, his own exhibits only upstairs.

"Why?"

In London, his raw strength had anchored her when she felt she might drift off into nothing. Somehow, he had connected her to life again. But now, that strength of his was dangerous to her. To Trish. Looking into his eyes, she knew a terrified conviction that her life—Trish's life—could slip from her control.

She turned and walked abruptly into her kitchen, pulled down the coffee grounds and started preparing the coffeemaker. She could feel him when he came into the kitchen. He made no sound, his white track shoes silent on her carpet. He had followed slowly from the living room, taking his time.

He said quietly, "Why are you afraid of me?"

Her hands jerked. The coffee grounds scattered across the white countertop. He took the cloth from her and she watched him cleaning the mess up. Abrupt. Efficient.

Nothing would stop him.

"You're frightening," she said quietly. She put the water into the coffeemaker and turned the machine on.

"You weren't afraid of me in London."

"No. That was..." Memories. Hidden memories. Never real. The man, the shadow, with no name. She said unsteadily, "Can I make you go away?"

"No."

Her heart crashed against her ribs. "So...what do you suggest we do now?"

"We could go out to dinner. There's that nightclub around the curve of the bay. Where your friend works. Or we could go into Duncan."

There was dancing at the nightclub. His arms around her. She would be lost if he held her, and she knew that going out was risky. Someone could walk up and say, "Hello and how's your daughter doing?" Then Ryan would ask about Trish and——

"Not dinner out." She crossed her arms, cupped her elbows in her palms and tried for a casual voice. "I'm not going out. I have this client who gives me a salmon almost every week. If I don't eat them, they fill my freezer and become a major problem. Especially as——"

"Especially as?"

She bit her lip. As Trish hates fish, she had almost said. "I barbecue them." She tried to steady her breathing. "Or fry them . . . bake them. They're always big monster fish, and I'll be glad when salmon season is over and I can go back to turkey and chicken."

He was amused. "You're inviting me to dinner here?"

Was she? She reached for mugs from a shelf. He reached, too, his hands closing on two mugs easily.

"Where is this client?"

"Campbell River. He's a fisherman." She took the mugs away from him, put them beside the coffeemaker.

"One of your bookkeeping clients?"

She sighed. "My mother? You've been talking about me with my mother?"

"Yes. I like Sarah. She's real." His lips twitched as if at a secret joke.

I'm not real, she almost said, except that even the thought brought an echo of his eyes on hers in the midst of a crowded room years ago and thousands of miles away. She said neutrally, "If you're staying, you'll have to deal with the barbecue."

"Fair enough," he agreed.

He went out onto the patio to look at it. She saw his back, a glimpse through the window. He called, "Okay, it's lit! I'm going to prowl around your garden."

She cut the fish into steaks. Two for him, because he was a big man, filled with quiet energy. He would have a hearty appetite. One salmon steak for her, and she hoped she could actually eat it. She had leftover rice in the fridge and she mixed diced, cooked carrots and onions with the rice, making it into balls in foil to warm on the barbecue. When she carried the food out to the table by the barbecue, he was out on the lawn, his hand curled around an old swing she had put up for a younger Trish.

"What are you working on now?" she asked.

"Shall I call you Gail?" he asked idly.

"No," she snapped, staring at him, knowing he was going to ask about the swing. Swings were for children.

"Abby, then?" The seat of the swing moved against his legs, struck against his calf. "Abby, but I'll always know you as Gail."

She shook her head.

His eyes changed. He said quietly, "You haven't said my name once. Not today. Not last week." He gave the empty swing a small push and moved away from it. "Tell me about your business. How did you start it? When?"

"I saved up, working in an accountant's office while I was studying for my own accounting qualification at night school. Then I bought a van and fitted it with a computer." She turned and put the salmon steaks on the barbecue. "I started a sort of mobile computer accounting service. Five years ago." The year Trish went away to school.

He nodded and she thought he already knew this. "I'd never have pictured you doing anything so mundane as keeping books, but you've found an unconventional way to do it, at least." Then he was behind her, close, leaning over her shoulder as he said, "Here, I'll tend to the cooking. I told you I would."

He took the turner from her fingers. She let go abruptly. "I'm not unconventional," she snapped.

"Aren't you, Gail?"

"My name's not Gail." Her heart smashed heavily against her ribs. "It's Abby."

"Your mother said——"

"You talk to my mother too much. No one's ever called me Gail."

"I called you Gail. In London."

The air between them crackled with hidden fire. She smoothed her hands on her jeans. "I...I have—about twenty clients. Small businesses, people who don't want to take their records into a city accounting office." She moved away from the grilling fish and toward the swing. She sat down, curled her hands around the ropes and pushed against the ground with her sandals. Anything but talk about London, about old memories. "My clients—I visit them all twice a month."

He turned a salmon steak. She watched his back rather than his hands. Disturbing, watching his hands. His back was broad and strong.

Her fingers spread out on his shoulders, the mystery of his dark flesh under her caress. Staring up and...

She swallowed, closed her eyes, jerked them open again. She would *not* remember that afternoon! All these years, and she had managed to keep it shadowy, dream stuff, forgotten with the morning.

He asked, "What about your daughter?" and she gasped, her hands clenching on the rope. He lowered the lid of the barbecue over the steaks. "They'll be done in a few moments," he told her.

Then he came across the grass toward her. He had discarded the jacket somewhere. The camera too, she had thought, but now it was in his hands. He lifted it and she looked away, not wanting to look into the lens, afraid that his film might see something hidden from his eyes. She pushed at the ground with her feet and swung faster, higher.

The camera clicked. He was behind her and she could hear the whirring noise as his camera wound itself. She *would not* turn, would not look, would not tell him to stop. She felt his hands on her back. Pushing her higher.

"Where is she, Gail?" he asked. "Your daughter."

She gripped the ropes tightly, closed her eyes and felt the dizzy spinning from his gentle push on her back. Swinging back and forth. Back to his touch burning through her blouse, then away. With her eyes closed, ears straining, she heard the camera again, clicking, whirring.

"Where is your daughter?"

"Ben's daughter," she corrected, no expression at all in her voice, her heart smashing rhythmically into her ribs. He must read the lie in her voice.

She swung back, expecting his touch, hands on her back pushing, but there was nothing. She dragged her sandals on the ground, ground the swing to a stop and lurched out of it, turning, disoriented and still dizzy from the motion, finding him there with his camera. She wanted to reach for the camera, open it and yank the film out, but she must never let him see how badly he unnerved her.

"How do you look after her when you're off on your trips?"

"She...goes to a boarding school." Abby saw the smoke rising from the barbecue and rushed toward it thankfully. "The salmon's done. I'll get the plates."

The Indian summer sun had gone behind a cloud, leaving the air cool. They took their dinner inside. Abby moved toward the dining room, but Ryan stopped at the breakfast bar in the kitchen, saying, "I'm not formal company. This is where you and your daughter eat, isn't it?''

"Yes," she agreed. "Tell me what you're working on now. Mom said you were in South America recently."

"Panama." It was easier then, because he did not seem to mind telling her about the book on Panama that he had just finished. "I don't know what's next. I'm just wandering around, waiting for it to grab me." He shrugged. "I go through this process. At first, it used to terrify me. I'd finish a project and feel rootless, cast out and convinced I'd never get another going. Now— well, I know it's part of the way I work. So I'm doing mundane stuff while I wait, some calendar pictures for one of your Canadian banks."

"Where do you live? London?"

"I've got a place down on the Baja—Mexico—that's as close to home as anything." His fingers turned his beer glass around and around. "I move around, cart my supplies after me, store things here and there. Every book is in a different country, so there doesn't seem much point to settling anywhere."

"A rootless life?"

His smile was mocking. "Perhaps I'm looking for something."

"Are you?" Her heart had begun to beat with a deep, throbbing pulse.

"Maybe it's you I've been looking for."

"I doubt it." Her voice was sharper than she intended. All those pictures in his book. She had known, turning the pages. She stood up and started clearing their plates. "I imagine your reasons are inside yourself, but blame me if you like. It makes no difference to me."

She did not want him helping her with the dishes, but he was there, asking where the dish towels were, drying plates, opening her cupboards and putting things away in the wrong places, then asking, "Are you going to show me around your home?"

"If you'll leave after I do." He shrugged and she should have known that was no answer, but moving was easier than being still with his gaze on her.

"Leave your camera behind," she said, and he smiled, but when she started the tour he had the camera slung over his shoulder, the black strap slashed against his red shirt. He looked good in red.

"You don't listen, do you?" she snapped. Then, "Dining room," she said, making the tour fast and abrupt. "Living room." She gestured toward the corridor to the back. "Bathroom. Bedrooms."

"Yours? Your daughter's?"

"Yes," she agreed, moving toward the stairs.

"I'd like to see them."

She felt her jaw jerk, moved past him and threw the doors open one by one. The chaos that was her own room, the tidy order of Trish's.

"Her name's Trish?"

"Patricia Benita," she corrected tensely.

"After her father?"

Oh, God! "Yes," she managed to say. She passed him, started up the stairs. He followed her up.

"My office is up here. Computer. Copies of clients' books. Business telephone." It rang as she said the words and she moved away from him, reaching for it.

She sank down to make notes as a garage-owner client started talking quickly and urgently into her ear. She tried not to be aware of the man prowling around the room, but she felt herself jerk when the camera went again. She wanted to scream at him, knew that would reveal more than anything else how badly he unnerved her.

If he ever realized how desperately she needed him to leave, he would want to know why. Now he was prowling along the edges of the room, looking at her sketches. Restless, filled with life. She had always seen that in him, even when he was motionless.

Always? As if...

"Yes," she said to Dennis on the telephone. "I think you can. Change their shifts. Put Ellie on with Brenda, because you're certain of her. Then cash up yourself at the end of the shift. Yes, that's right. Then I'll give you the daily stats related to shifts from last month when I'm up there next."

"Employee pilfering?" he asked as she hung up.

"Yes." She tore off her page of notes, opened a file drawer and slipped them into Dennis's folder.

"All in a day's work?"

She ground out, "Don't take any more pictures of me. I don't like it."

His eyes laughed at her.

"If I find pictures of me in one of your books," she threatened, "I'll sue you."

She gasped as he moved abruptly close. He touched her face and she could not stop the instinct that made her jerk back.

"Gail, if I wanted to circulate pictures of you, I've got lots of them." Her eyes widened and he said softly, "The pictures I have of you are far more revealing than anything I've gotten today."

Pictures. His camera. All these years, and somehow she had insanely believed that none of it would be real, that it was all so foggy and unreal that nothing could come of it. She closed her eyes painfully.

Not real, except for Trish, and even that had seemed dissociated. With Hans enshrining Ben, standing as godfather and reminding her almost weekly of what Benedict would have wanted for his child. *His child.*

She looked desperately around the room, then at the man. "That's all there is to the house. You've seen it." She turned and walked away from him, toward the stairs.

"I heard that you were a groupie." He was standing at the wall, fingers almost touching a sketch she had done of an old truck left abandoned in the trees somewhere on northern Vancouver Island. He said quietly, "Benedict Stakeman's wife. A student of his with no talent. Grasping for the echo of fame."

She swallowed painfully. "You...gossiped about me?"

"Heard gossip," he corrected. "And I didn't know it was you." He looked from the sketch to Abby, then back again. "Did you hang around galleries all the time? That's how you met me. Is that how you met him? Did you meet him that weekend?"

"No."

He moved to another sketch. A log cabin built so far back in time that there was no roof left, hardly even walls. The forest had grown back to reclaim its own. Only an echo left of the dreamer who had built a home there in the trees.

She said, "Those sketches aren't——"

"Aren't what?" he demanded, moving to the next one.

"They're for me. Just for me." She moved closer to him, her hand going out, then falling back to touch her thigh as she realized how silly it was. Trying to protect them from him. "Don't criticize them."

He was almost smiling. "But that's almost the first thing you said to me—criticism of my work."

"But you know damned well you're good. And these— I didn't marry Ben because of his painting. I——" She shrugged, and surprised herself by admitting, "Maybe I did, partly. Hero worship." It seemed so far back in the past. "The part about my having no talent, that was true. I took a class from him. A night class. That's how we met. And——" He could easily ask *when*. If he started checking up on dates, she knew exactly what conclusions he would come to. She pushed that thought back, afraid he might see it in her eyes. "You don't need to tell me these are just doodles."

"Doodles?"

She waved the sketches away. "I know they're nothing special. I do them for me. Not for anyone else. Why do you think they're up here, not downstairs."

His brows were lifted and he moved almost angrily from one sketch to the other. "No talent," he muttered. "Did he tell you that?"

"Look, I—— Why should I have to defend my hobbies to you? To anyone?" She pushed her hair back and felt the knot of it at her nape starting to give way. He would never go, never leave her alone. She muttered, "If I wanted to knit in my spare time, you wouldn't glare at the sweaters I made and mutter about talent and a waste of time. Would you?"

He swung toward her and she saw his hands go out. She gasped as they closed on her arms. He ground out, "You're a bloody fool if you think these are *doodles*. Anyone with half a brain can see what you've done here. You've caught a world, a way of life."

"I can sketch, that's all. Coordination, nothing more." She shook her head angrily. "I've got no sense of color, and those are just..."

"What do you think makes an artist? Skillful hands? Technique? Art is in the eyes, in sight." His fingers curled into her upper arms. When she winced, he let her free abruptly. His jaw jerked. "I always heard he was pompous, but trying to suppress the kind of talent you've got is a crime."

She said stiffly, "There's not much point to our talking about the past, is there?"

Suddenly the anger left him. "Our past," he said in a low voice. "Say my name, Gail."

She shook her head mutely, staring up at him with her lips pressed tightly together. "I'll make you," he threatened softly.

"Don't touch me." She thought she kept her voice steady, although inside there was a drugging helplessness crawling over her. She shuddered when he moved closer.

He threaded his fingers into her hair until they were caught by the tightly pulled twist. He was too close, standing in front of her, the cotton of his shirt brushing against her breasts when he shifted. His chest was rising and falling in a slow, steady pattern. "What are you doing?" she whispered.

"Letting your hair free." His voice was low, seductive. "Looking for the Gail I remember."

She shook her head and he slid his fingers under her chin. Like the cat, she thought, but she would not purr. He slid the clasp out of her hair. She heard the soft sound of it falling to the carpet. Memories. Sensations she had forgotten. Surely they were buried, gone.

His fingers slid through the fine length of her hair. She could feel the touch on her scalp, the movement of his thumbs massaging the nape of her neck and the hair sliding over his hands, over her shoulders, alive with his touch.

"I'm going to kiss you," he whispered huskily.

She made herself stare wide-eyed into his multicolored eyes. Hazel, it was called, but on him the colors were alive. Pulsing with promises. Threats. He brushed her lips with his.

"Say my name," he demanded again. His hands spread the hair out so that it cascaded over her shoulders. Then, and only then, he took her glasses away and laid them aside. "Gail," he whispered, "look at me."

She tried to look away then, but it was too late. His trap. His voice. His hands caressing the shining fall of her hair, sliding under and coming up around her throat in a parody of a lovers' caress. He bent to take the trembling at her throat under his lips and the sound jammed up in her throat, but she kept the whisper of a sigh locked in.

"Yes," he said in a hypnotic whisper. "I see it in your eyes." He linked his fingers with hers and drew her with him. He caught at the strap of his camera and put it somewhere behind him. The little coffee table, she thought, trying to hold on to that detail as a symbol of reality. His gaze remained locked with hers as he drew her down, taking her with him until they were sitting on the deep sofa and his hands were in her hair, on her face, bringing her close for his kiss.

"You were in the crowd," he said in a voice she had to strain to hear.

She could feel the crowd around her, the noises, the smoke. She saw this man, and knew that he was the only reality.

He said, "I saw you and we both knew. You waited there for me to come to you. Your eyes were wide and staring, holding mine." He brushed the curtain of hair away from one shoulder. "Say my name, Gail."

She pressed her lips together, but his voice would not stop, its low tones curling around her nerves until she thought she would scream. "I told you my name that day." His thumb brushed across her lower lip. "I remember my name on your lips. You whispered it. All those people, all that noise, but I would have heard you anywhere. You were...almost unreal. I had the strangest feeling...as if when I took your hand and led you to my studio you were the one taking me away from reality, into dreams."

She saw his gaze drop to her mouth, saw the deep lines that curved at either side of his mouth, the solid thrust of his chin.

"I kissed you that day, sitting on my sofa." His lips brushed hers. "Soft," he whispered. "You were so soft." He found the line of her jaw, the softness below her ear. "You were wearing silver earrings that day. Long, dangly strands of silver caressing your neck."

She shook her head, but his voice seduced her memory. He had taken them out of her ears, his hand fumbling gently on her flesh. "Not like these ones," he murmured, freeing her ear of one gold hoop, then another. "More...insubstantial. Caressing your neck. You left them behind," he said huskily. "I found them after you were gone."

She could never have worn them again.

His mouth took the softness of her earlobe prisoner as his fingers traced along the trembling white of her throat. She felt his fingers on her buttons.

CHAPTER FIVE

"LAST time," he said steadily, his fingers caressing her throat, "last time you were the one who reached to free your buttons."

Her eyes widened and he said huskily, "Yes. You remember, don't you? You wore a long blue dress with a pleated skirt and a button bodice. You hair was drifting all around, and there were little buttons from your neck down to your waist. I thought I would never breathe again, watching you free them one by one."

Three buttons, he had said, so that he could take her picture. He had watched with eyes so dark that they were more than black. She had been frozen, only her fingers moving.

"This time," he breathed, leaning over her on her own sofa, "this time I'll do it." She felt his fingers. Her blouse was long-sleeved, loose over her jeans. Blue, as the dress had been.

"One," he said musingly. She felt the back of his knuckles against her breastbone. There was nowhere to pull back, just the softness of her own sofa. No words to stop him.

"Two." His knuckles brushed just above the softness.

A band tightened around her chest and he knew. His fingers brushed deliberately against the swelling. She should jerk away. Run out of this house, next door. Anywhere. Away from him.

Sandra, she thought wildly, but Sandra would be no protection at all.

He bent his head and she was staring at the casual wave of his black hair while she clenched her hands into fists in her lap.

"Last time the buttons were closer together," he mused, his fingers poised on the third one. "Say my name, Gail."

Memories...

"Say my name."

His face dark over hers, his eyes delving deeply into hers.

"Ryan," she whispered.

"No!" she gasped now.

He freed the button. A blouse this time, not the dress. He brushed it aside and she could feel the cool air on her flesh. He was staring at her, whispering, "I remember this...so white...soft."

This could not be happening. She could not sit here, motionless, *letting* him slowly strip away her...her clothing...the veil over her memories. He touched the fabric of her bra and she tried to fight the sensations surging up, the part of her that needed to melt closer into his arms, to raise her lips to his, let him bend down and take her where there was no pain, no ice.

She gasped as his fingers brushed the hard peak of her breast through the lacy covering of her bra. "Yes," he insisted. "You remember." He taunted the hardness to aching sensitivity. Remember. She felt the tears welling up even as a pulse throbbed deep inside her. Somehow, she kept her body rigid.

"Are you going to take me?" she whispered.

His free hand caught her chin and forced her to meet his eyes. No softness, although he had kissed her throat gently only a moment ago. "Whatever you'll give," he said softly. She could feel his touch, still gentle, curved around her swollen woman's breast.

She was going to cry. Now, with him watching.

He said quietly, "I could have you. You wouldn't stop me." She would not answer...could not. He held her gaze for what seemed eternity, then abruptly she was free. "And you'd be gone tomorrow," he finished without inflection. "As you were the last time."

She sat stiffly with her blouse fallen around her, the fabric pooled around her arms. "My body. That's all you had the last time." A lie, and he knew it. She could feel seductive sensations crawling across her skin. He was so close, his thigh touching hers. "I wouldn't stop you," she admitted.

His touch still throbbed in her. She remembered that, the pulsing deep inside. Something primitive and frightening, cravings he knew he could rouse in her.

She whispered, "If you—if——"

He reached out his hand and her whole body went into a spasm of aching. His thumb brushed her cheek, then lightly across her long eyelashes. He said, "I remember that look in your eyes. Haunted." His thumb slid down along her cheek, her throat. Her blouse was still undone and she tried to tell her fingers to move, pull it up, fasten the buttons, make barriers. He said gently, "It tore at me, knowing you were hurting. I tried...I told myself I wouldn't push you. Just hold you, and...I thought we had time."

"We never had time," she whispered. "Never."

She thought wildly that if she moved into his arms he would stop asking questions, his eyes would close and stop trying to pry. She remembered...

Nothing! She remembered nothing.

"Say my name, Gail." His hands cupped her face, fingers spreading back into her hair. "Say my name, love, or I'll kiss you again." His face moved closer, so that she could feel his words breathing on her mouth. "And this time," he promised, "I won't stop until you're begging me to take off more than the blouse."

She gasped, "I didn't...beg you."

"Don't you remember?"

She clenched her hands into hard knots in her lap. "Ryan," she whispered. "Ryan. Is that what you want?" He was silent and she opened her eyes. His were hazel again. Remote, not hot, and, although she might have tried to make it otherwise, he had always been Ryan.

He said tonelessly, "I promise that my name on your lips is only the beginning." He slid the fabric of her blouse back up her arms, adjusting it on her shoulders, not buttoning it.

She felt unsteady when she stood. She walked to the window and stared down at the driveway below. A Porsche. Gray. Powerful. She wondered if he had rented it or bought it. Wondered when he would leave and knew she would feel pain, watching that car drive away with him at the wheel.

She said unsteadily, "You can't come tomorrow."

"You need breathing space?" Was he laughing? How had he known her body would turn lethargic and unsteady when he touched her?

"Yes," she agreed. "Not...tomorrow." An affair, she thought wildly. Somewhere else. Not here. Somewhere they could be...anonymous.

"Saturday, then," he said. "I'll come Saturday morning."

She swung around, panicked. "You can't."

"Why not?"

She rubbed her palms down along her jeans, realized that her buttons were still undone, her blouse hanging open. She fumbled with the buttons, caught between turning away from his eyes and the knowledge that if he caressed her with those clever, gentle hands she would lose track of the world again.

She admitted, "Because Trish will be here." He would twist secrets from her lips if he knew they were there. She would not be able to stop him.

"I want to meet her."

"I don't want you to meet her." She jerked her head, sending her fair hair flying back behind her shoulders. "Hans Bunian. He—he's Trish's godfather. He's coming to look at her work. And my mother and—they'll all be here. You can't—I'll—I know we—I'll meet you somewhere."

"I'll come Saturday."

"Why? What do you want?" She felt swollen, aching. Looking in his eyes, she thought it showed. As if she were naked, her heart and her thoughts stripped while he watched.

"I want to understand."

She swallowed. "You mean—why I married Ben?"

He shrugged. "Maybe I just need to know why I give a damn after all these years."

She said abruptly, "I married Ben before." She saw him jerk, sucked in a deep breath and added, "Before I met you."

"You were married when you met me? You weren't wearing a ring."

"No." She turned back to the window. "Ben didn't believe in rings. Trappings of a society he rejected."

He laughed cynically. "There wasn't a damned painter alive who cared more about what the world thought than Benedict Stakeman."

"I know," she admitted.

In a hard voice, he demanded, "And you? What did you believe in? Not faithfulness?"

His accusation was not true, but the truth was impossible. "What do you want me to say?"

"My name," he suggested harshly. "So I know you're not blending me with a thousand other men, other afternoons. What's my name?"

"Ryan," she whispered. "And there was no one else."

"He was downstairs. His showing downstairs. Mine upstairs."

"Yes," she agreed.

"And you came upstairs. With your husband downstairs." She heard his angry movement. "Look at me, damn you!"

It did not matter if he hated her. The important thing was for him to go away. Never to come back. She told herself that, although there was pain in her heart.

His words were only a growl, hurled angrily toward her. "While I was waiting for you, were you with him?"

She stared back at him, afraid she could not make the lie work if her lips moved. His hands tightened on her arms. Hard. She welcomed the pain and tried to keep her eyes wide and blank.

"And the day before," he growled, "you were with me. In my arms. In my bed." She shivered and he said grimly, "Naked, in my arms, loving with me." His voice sharpened and he shook her slightly, demanded, "Was he waiting for you while you were with me?"

She made her mind blank, hoped her eyes reflected nothing.

"Answer me, damn you!" He released her and she almost stumbled.

"I don't have to answer you. I don't have to tell you anything."

She walked past him, down the stairs. His jacket was lying across her living room sofa. He was behind her, following her. She picked the jacket up and held it out to him.

"Saturday," he said. "Expect me on Saturday."

"No. Not Saturday. I'll meet you somewhere. Anywhere you want, but not here. I don't want you to come here."

His mouth turned into a hard line. She could feel the anger underneath, although his voice was cold as he said softly, "I don't give a damn, Gail. I'll be here."

She could feel her heart pounding harder with every beat. Fear, all the more oppressive because it was intangible, because she did not know exactly what terrible thing would happen if he learned the truth.

She had only one weapon, one terrible lie that she had lived for years already. He opened the door, looked back to lift his hand, a casual wave, as if he were her friend.

She said, "You asked about Ben. And London. I'll tell you if you have to know." He froze, motionless, waiting, and, before his gaze could actually lock on her, she said the words.

"I was carrying his child when I was with you." She closed her eyes and lied on a harsh whisper, "Ask anyone, because it was no secret. It was announced the day—day before..."

He must have believed her lie, because he turned and he was gone.

She pushed the door closed, then she locked it, and if he heard the lock slamming home she was glad. Her hands were shaking so badly.

But why was she crying?

On Saturday morning, Abby's mother and Damian came first. Abby heard the bell and went to the door, peeking through the window in case there was a gray Porsche outside. Crazy, because he would never be back now.

She had always hated scenes. She liked calm. Quiet. That was why she had felt such a sick pain when he left. That must be why she had let the tears come, or perhaps the tears were old ones that should have been let go years ago.

Say my name.

Ryan.

"Morning, dear." Her mother's cheek was cool from the September air. Abby hugged her, amused because they were both wearing beige pants. She smiled at Damian, who was standing behind her mother. Although he could be quietly difficult, she had liked her stepfather from the first time she met him. He was restrained, practical, and he loved her mother.

Today he was dressed in his version of leisure wear—lightweight formal trousers and an open-necked shirt under an expensive wool sweater in a dark, restrained color, gray hair and a conservative smile over it all. He always looked like the banker he was, even in a swimsuit.

"How's our girl?" asked Sarah, shedding her wool jacket as she came through the door.

Abby grimaced. "She's out back, either swinging or wrecking the backyard. We had a royal battle last night. She doesn't want to show Hans her portfolio. This morning, over breakfast, she informed me coldly that she intended to run away from home. In the end she settled for dressing in fluorescent striped yellow Lycra biker shorts, which she believes will shock Hans."

Damian winced and Sarah laughed. "What's she wearing on top?"

"A bright green skintight T-shirt. I'm hoping the visual violence will satisfy her, and that she won't say anything to make Hans lose his temper."

"Shall I talk to her?" suggested Damian.

"Yes, please," said Abby gratefully. "She might actually listen to you, which would be something between a miracle and impossible. If you could make her see that life would be much easier without Hans creating an artistic tantrum all over us..." Abby spread her hands helplessly. "I've lost my cool entirely. If she tells you her mother's a wild shrew, it's true."

He laughed and she grimaced. "While you're out there, I'll try to find out from my own mother what it is I'm supposed to do when my daughter turns into a yellow striped monster."

Sarah said, "The only thing you can do. Wait it out." Damian was laughing gently as he left. "The best thing about Damian," said Sarah, "is that he doesn't take insults seriously."

Abby sighed. "I hope your granddaughter isn't such a brat that she'd insult her grandfather, but today I won't guarantee it."

"Damian's difficult to insult. And deceptively stubborn. What are you planning for lunch? Something I can help with?"

"Sandwiches." She led her mother into the kitchen where the sandwiches were piled high on a covered plate. "Hans is an erratic eater, and I'm not sure how long he's going to stay. Not long, I hope. I got French wine. It's the only thing he'll drink."

"Difficult man." Sarah lifted the cover on the sandwiches. "Enough, do you think? Or should I do a few more? And if you don't want Hans here, why let him come?"

"He was Ben's best friend. And he's been wonderful with Trish. It's just that Trish is so unsettled lately, and...well, he sets her off with his determination to be her artistic mentor. The timing is rotten, that's all. And— That's Hans at the door. I recognize his knock."

* * *

This time, when Ryan drove into Abby's drive, there were cars everywhere. Damian Rule's Chrysler. Abigail's van. The battered Lotus that must belong to Hans Bunian.

No one came to the front door when he knocked. Ryan could hear sounds from the back. He opened the door and went into the house. He found the tabby cat lying on the mat just inside the door. No one else.

"Hi, kitty," he said softly, scratching its ear when it stretched up to greet him. "Are they all out back?"

The cat's purr shifted gears. He said, "I know. She told me not to come." He thought of leaving, now, before she saw him. He was not sure he wanted to meet the daughter either, could feel his gut tighten at the thought. The child Gail had been carrying when...

"Tabby, my girl, avoiding unpleasant things doesn't get a man anywhere."

He walked through her empty house to the backyard.

He saw Gail first. Abby, he corrected, watching her sitting in the swing, moving gently back and forth, her head tilted slightly as if she were listening to something Damian was saying with careful concentration. She was wearing beige pants and a matching blouse that made her look pale and subdued. As Ryan watched, Sarah came up to them and rested her hand on Damian's shoulder. Abby said something that looked rueful and Sarah laughed.

All three of them looked toward Ryan's left.

Bunian was there, dressed in drooping gray pants and an ancient, expensive suit jacket. Above the gray, his hair stuck out wild and white. His voice droned in a strong, endless tirade. "Callman is inadequate," he was saying loudly, staring down at something in front of him. Ryan saw the man's arm come down around a small shoulder under curly, dark hair.

She must be eleven, her thin back drowned by Bunian's heavy arm. Ryan did not want to do the arithmetic, but it was automatic, counting from some time not too long before that afternoon in London. Not long before, because Gail—Abby—had been in his arms and there had been no sign of... Damn! He hated the thought! As if she had been his, and Stakeman was the man she'd been unfaithful with. He knew it was irrational, he had no right to resentment. Stakeman might have had a right, except that Ryan could remember how Gail's eyes had looked trapped on film, and none of it made sense.

Bunian's voice dragged on. "Light and shade...perspective...nobody could be so stupid as to think that sketch has any resemblance to the real animal."

The girl's shoulders were rigid. She turned, pulling away from the painter's arm. Those yellow striped pants were shocking, painful to the eyes. Ryan almost laughed as he saw Bunian wince as he looked at the girl. The bright T-shirt clung to her thin form, clashing wildly with the pants. Then Ryan saw her eyes, the suppressed tears she refused to give way to.

Green eyes. Deep and alive with anger and hurt. Eyes too big for her thin face. She was thin all over, tall for her age, all tension and difficult emotions hidden inside. That wild, dark mop of hair and those green eyes defied the world.

He recognized her.

"You what?" gasped Abby, staring at Damian. She curled her fingers around the swing and felt the motion under her.

Her stepfather shrugged, amusement showing in his eyes. "I told her if she didn't like what Hans was saying—ignore it."

Sarah's hand rested on Damian's shoulder. "That's my husband. No respect for art."

Abby eyed Trish uneasily. The girl had been quiet since Damian's talk with her. She had greeted Hans quite affectionately, but right now, watching them—Abby could not hear the words, just Hans's voice rumbling on and on.

Suddenly, Trish pulled away from Hans and spun around. Abby winced when she saw her daughter's face. She stood up abruptly and started across the lawn toward Trish.

"Damian," said Sarah. "You'd better..."

Trish's jaw was working. Hans said something derogatory about Callman's skills as a teacher, then growled, "You'll come to me this Christmas. Six hours a day, and I'll get rid of those habits he's let you develop."

Trish said nothing, but Abby could feel the quiet explosion coming. She broke in hurriedly, "Hans, Christmas isn't possible. Trish and I are going to Hawaii with Mom and Damian." She put her arm around Trish, felt her daughter twisting away, tension radiating from her in waves.

Abby turned toward Hans, then froze abruptly, her eyes widening.

Ryan!

He was moving between Trish and Hans, turning his back on Hans, reaching toward the drawings on the picnic table. Abby heard her own voice squeak his name.

"That's Tabby, isn't it?" he asked, his gaze swinging toward Trish. Trish glared at him, but Abby thought she relaxed slightly as Ryan asked, "Is that what she looked like when you found her?"

Hans demanded grimly, "Who the hell are you?"

Ryan did not even look at Hans as he answered, "Ryan Marsdon."

Hans echoed, "Marsdon? My God, yes! You did that incredible Iraqi study?"

Ryan was not even listening to Hans. To Trish, he said, "May I look at the other pictures?"

The girl wrapped thin arms around her waist and muttered, "I don't care."

He studied the next sketch. "So it snows here in the winter. I'd wondered."

Trish nodded. "Sometimes. Not always, but that's why I had to bring Tabby home. Because winter comes."

"Yes," he agreed with a smile. He shuffled the sketches together into a tidy pile, then slipped them back into the portfolio.

Hans said heavily, "Trish and I were conferring on her work."

"You're finished," Ryan said quietly. He handed the portfolio to Trish. She clutched it tightly to her thin young body.

Hans's face was swelling with anger, glowing red. "You've no right to interfere between me and my god-daughter!"

Abby was frozen, watching in horror, a knot of disaster growing, clamping down on her throat and locking her gaze on the man who was the cause of Hans's fury. Ryan Marsdon. There was no way he could know the truth. No way at all. But he swung his head and she saw his eyes.

Hans reached for Trish's portfolio. Ryan blocked him. "Put it away, Trish," he said quietly. He held Hans's gaze in a battle of wills, said softly, "I'd suggest you go away and think about what an eleven-year-old girl is all about."

Behind him, Trish's voice said quietly, "I'm only ten, but I'll be eleven soon."

Abby saw the harshness leave his eyes. He asked carefully, "When's your birthday? December?"

"You're a good guesser." Trish almost grinned. "Christmas Eve."

Abby was a block of ice, waiting for the next blow to fall, because it was in Ryan's eyes. There was no way he would turn and walk away now. She could feel Hans gearing up for a full explosion, but when he erupted she thought Ryan would snap right back with *his* weapon. They would fight their battle in her backyard, tearing apart the fabric of her life.

Sarah said placatingly, "Hans, I think maybe——"

"Shut up!" bellowed Hans.

Sarah gasped and Damian murmured something soothing.

Hans growled, "This child must be handled *properly*." His finger swung to jab toward Ryan. "You, sir! I respect your talent, but this is *not* your affair! If you are a *friend* of Abby's, you can be sure I will talk to her about——"

"That's enough." Ryan's voice was quiet, but Hans broke off as if he had been slapped. Abby felt like a spectator in a movie theater as Ryan said casually, "Trish and I are going for a walk. I imagine she's had enough of art for one day. I certainly have." He caught Abby's eyes, said softly, "I think Abby could tell you that I've every right to interfere."

He turned away. "Coming?" he asked Trish.

She held the portfolio tightly to her chest as she stepped away from Hans. Neither Ryan nor Trish said a word as they walked into the house, leaving four adults speechless.

Abby heard Damian mutter something softly to Sarah, then a sound suspiciously like suppressed laughter.

Damian started to say something tactful, but Abby interrupted. "Hans, I think you should go." Her voice was thick and awkward, the words forced because Ryan had meant every word.

I've every right to interfere.

Rights? Did he have rights? Could he prove——?

Damian slipped between Abby and Hans, started easing Hans tactfully toward the front door. Hans muttered and grumbled, while Sarah said something low and cautious to Abby. The words could not penetrate the roaring in Abby's ears.

She had woken so often with restless memories of an afternoon in London that made her life since seem pale and empty in comparison. And yet, for all the dreams, she had never fantasized Ryan walking in, threatening to blow her life wide-open, talking about rights.

CHAPTER SIX

SHE found them on the beach. Trish was a brilliant splash of striped, fluorescent yellow down near the water. Ryan was sitting, leaning back against a big rock, watching. He saw Abby coming. She crammed her hands into the pockets of her beige pants and kept walking toward him.

She asked, "How did you know?"

He shrugged. "I could show you a picture of my younger sister. You'd think it was Trish in the picture."

"I didn't know you had a sister."

He said quietly, "I didn't know you had my daughter."

She tried to stop the trembling, but when she made fists of her hands in her pockets, she could feel shaken fear inside. "You're angry."

"Yes." He looked at the brilliant colors of the girl down by the water. "*Our daughter* is notorious. A legend. Patricia Benita Stakeman. The daughter Benedict Stakeman never lived to see. Hans Bunian's prodigy. You've got that child living a lie." He scooped up a small handful of fine sand. "How could you tell everyone it was his child growing inside you?" He opened his fingers slightly and the sand and gravel slid out in a soft stream.

"I didn't..." She choked a sob back. "I didn't tell anyone. Ben—he announced—the night of the accident, he'd told——"

"You knew it was my child."

"Yes!" Down at the water's edge, Trish saw her mother and waved. Abby waved back, closed her eyes and lowered her voice to a whisper. "What are you going to do?"

87

"That's up to you."

"What do you mean?" She looked at him then, but his eyes frightened her. "Ryan——"

"I'm that girl's father. I intend to be in her life. And I want Hans Bunian out. For the rest..." He shrugged. "The main thing is, you'll keep Bunian away from her, or I'll tell him exactly whose daughter he's trying to turn into an impressionist echo of reality."

She shuddered. He was not joking. "What can I tell Hans?"

"Lies," he suggested wryly. "You're good at lies."

It would never work. One day the truth would burst out. If Ryan had never come back, never seen Trish, the secret might have lain buried forever. If...

Somehow she would have to tell them all herself. Hans, frightening though he could be, might just be possible. Under the rough exterior, Hans was a warm and caring man. She thought she could bring herself to tell Hans. And her mother.

But Trish?

Ryan said, "I've wanted you a long time," his voice sliding over her flesh. He saw the shock in her widening eyes. "Think about it," he suggested. "It's your choice."

She swallowed painfully and knew the tears were too close. "You mean... you want me to... be your——"

"Lover?" He stood up and brushed the sand from his jeans. "Maybe. I know I used to want you quite badly. As for now—I'll have to think about it." The soft threat in his voice echoed in her long after he had gone, and Abby shuddered as she watched her daughter playing down on the water's edge.

Abby's mother phoned late the next Thursday afternoon. "How was your business trip?" she asked. Then, in the next breath, "You didn't tell me you'd been seeing Ryan Marsdon."

"I'm not," protested Abby. She twisted a long strand of hair around her finger and shifted the telephone on her shoulder. "We're not seeing each other."

"Oh? What about the way he handled Hans last weekend! And about time, too, I'd say. Poor Trish has had enough of this embryonic-great-artist stuff. Where were you on Sunday? I called."

"Trish and I went to Duncan." She swallowed, tried to line up the words. *Trish is Ryan's child.*

"With Ryan?"

"Yes," admitted Abby. He had come knocking on her door on Sunday morning, dressed in jeans and a sweater against the wind, his eyes neutral. Trish had grinned when she saw him and even Abby had felt her day turning brighter despite the fact that he was danger to her. Lunch at McDonald's and a drive out to Lake Cowichan.

Afterward, he had driven Trish back to school, had let Abby off at her own front door. "Good night, Abigail," he had said softly. Not goodbye.

"Good night," she had echoed. She had climbed out of the Porsche and turned her back on him, had fumbled her keys because she knew that if she turned back...

London could happen all over again. It was still there. Everything. Emotions and need, pulsing in the air.

The next morning, Abby had packed her van and headed north on her rounds. The fisherman. The farmer. The toy shop. She had talked to the owners of the businesses she tended, had typed data into the computer in the back of her van, had looked over her shoulder more than once, her hands trembling. Insane to feel that he still wanted her badly enough to come looking. All these years, and he must have had countless women.

He had crawled out of her dreams and had started haunting her life.

He called on Thursday night. Abby had finished talking to her mother, had failed to make her confession. All week she had told herself that she had to tell everyone, that only the truth could end this fear she had of Ryan exploding the stability of her life with Trish. But, despite her vow to tell all, she had remained silent through the conversation with Sarah.

When the telephone rang, she knew it would be him.

He announced briskly, "I'll pick Trish up from school for you this weekend. Just give me directions on what to do when I get there."

Abby clenched the receiver. "No. I can pick her up."

She could hear the shrug in his voice. "That would be a waste of your time. I'm in Duncan in any case, and I'm coming out there. Don't bother cooking supper ahead. Trish and I will pick up some pizza and bring it out with us."

"What if we had other plans for the evening?"

"Have you?" She thought he was smiling, and that must mean he knew exactly what happened to her pulse when he was near.

"No," she admitted. "No other plans." She had never been good at lies. As a child, she had often confessed to childish sins she might well have got away with. It was ironic that she had been living a lie for over eleven years.

"So I'll pick her up. You can go out sketching this afternoon instead of coming into town."

"All right," she agreed. She needed to quieten her mind before she could meet him. A few hours spent with her sketchbook would do more for her than any other remedy.

She spent the afternoon over at the marina, trying to trap the atmosphere of the place on paper. Doodles, Ben had called them, but Ryan said she had talent. No, she thought, but it soothed her to narrow her eyes and worry how to catch the strange feeling of hard work and sweat she felt looking at the men on the deck of the fishing boat... the breathless adventure of the girl leaping on to the sailboat at the fuel float...the mundane day-after-day weariness of the fuel attendant as he moved out to serve his customers.

She was walking back around the curve of the bay when she heard the quiet purr of a powerful car crawling along the gravel road. With the brisk wind of early October twisting through her hair, it seemed easy to stick out her thumb as if she were a hiker angling for a ride.

Ryan rolled down his window. "Want a ride, lady?" Beside him, Trish giggled.

Abby shrugged indolently and scrambled into the back seat behind them, laughing when Trish said with mock severity, "Mommy, you mustn't take rides from strangers!"

"Watch out for strangers," agreed Ryan.

Strangers. London. Her hand in his, going where he led, into the room where his pictures surrounded them with war and pain. Memories. They surged over her and she caught frantically at the clasp at the back of her hair with one hand, jerking to free the hair. It flowed around her head, burying her face in a blond curtain. She caught it with both hands, smoothed it back, her head down, frowning as she concentrated on twisting her hair back into its bonds.

"I can smell the pizza," she said casually. "I'm starved."

"Good," Ryan said. Abby saw him grin at Trish.

Over their impromptu dinner, Abby could see that Trish was more relaxed than she had been in months. Ryan laughed and joked with Trish, teasing details of her school life out of her. The whole dinner went on at two levels. On the surface, laughter and easy conversation. Even Abby managed to answer Ryan's questions about the house, her job, her weekend activities, without sounding stilted. But underneath was the awareness of waiting. Marking time.

When Tabby came mewing at the front door, Trish went to let her in.

Ryan said quietly to Abby, "I've been looking up dates," and the abrupt change of subject shocked Abby. "Your husband died the day before you met me in that gallery."

Abby put her pizza piece back down on her plate.

He asked, "Had you just come from the hospital, when I first saw you at the gallery?"

"No. From the hotel." She could hear Trish crooning to Tabby in the next room. She twisted her ringless fingers together.

"Tell me," he demanded softly.

"When they sent me away from the hospital, I...some time in the night...I went to the hotel...flowers there. From Ben." She shivered from the old coldness. "I thought at the gallery I could be quiet and somehow...but there were so many people there. I went upstairs."

She could see Ryan's hands lying inert on the table. Perhaps she only imagined the tension, because his voice was toneless. "When we made love...were you pretending I was him?"

She had tried, but it was not Ben in her uncomfortable dreams. She looked up and of course it was anger in his eyes. He said slowly, "You pretended Trish was his child, because he was obsessed with wanting a child."

"No," she whispered, but he did not seem to hear.

His gaze scorned her with a weary cynicism. He said, "Her father can be whoever you say," and she saw his mouth turn hard as he warned, "But don't try to stop my seeing her. And I meant it about Bunian."

"He's her godfather. Hans loves her."

"I want him out of her life. Get the pressure off her. She's ten years old, too young to have all this pressure on her about her art."

"Ryan, I can't just—Hans is—I know he's bull-headed, but he does care about her. And she loves him." She saw the anger flash in his eyes, said hurriedly, "I know she hates the business about his critiquing her work, and I *have* talked to him about that. I called him this week. He's . . . agreed not to bring up her art to her for the time being."

His eyelids drooped over whatever emotion flashed in his eyes. Whatever he might have said in response was held back as he saw Trish coming into the kitchen with the kitten cuddled against her shoulder.

"How's Tabby?" asked Ryan.

"Okay," said Trish. "But hungry. Can she have some pizza?"

"Give her some of mine," volunteered Abby. "But not here. Outside on the porch."

Ryan pushed his chair back. "Are you two actually going to Hawaii this Christmas?"

Trish giggled. "That was a lie. Mommy told Uncle Hans that because he was hassling me and she said I deserve a holiday at Christmas."

Lies. Abby flushed and turned away from Ryan's gaze, heard him saying to Trish, "Then come to my place. I've got a house on the beach in Mexico."

"We can't," snapped Abby, but Trish was crushing Tabby tight, her green eyes lit with excitement. "We can't," repeated Abby flatly.

"Trish is welcome to come alone if you can't make it."

She could never let Trish go alone. What if Ryan never let her come back?

He would not do that to her. Of course not. He led a wandering life. The last thing he would want would be a permanent daughter. Hadn't he said that, back in London? That the last thing he wanted was chains.

"That's settled then," he said with satisfaction. "I'll arrange tickets for all three of us."

Later, he read Trish her bedtime story while Abby moved restlessly in the kitchen. She had put the pizza boxes in the bin, washed their plates and glasses. She went into the living room and was waiting for Ryan when he came out of Trish's room. She had his jacket in her hands.

"In a hurry for me to go?" His eyes were amused.

"Yes," she agreed.

His eyes darkened from hazel to flame. He took the jacket from her and laid it across the back of the sofa. She moved away as he came closer. One step. Two. She came up against the doorjamb. He reached out and caught a tendril of hair that had escaped the knot at the back of her neck.

"Afraid, Abigail?"

"Yes," she admitted.

"Of me?" He shook his head, seeing the answer in her eyes. "No. Of losing control?" he speculated. His voice was husky as he twisted the long golden strand around and around his finger. "I remember your hair loose and shining. Gold and shadows. You stared up at me. I saw your eyes change color as I stroked the softness of your hair."

"I don't remember." She remembered every second, every touch. Her own body lying naked and vulnerable in his arms. The image was sudden and shattering. She repeated, "I . . . remember *nothing*."

His gaze wandered down along the curve of her throat, caught at the pulse beating nervously there. He reached, traced her cheek lightly with his finger. She jerked back and came abruptly against the door.

"I don't believe you, Abigail. But we'll play your game if you like." He threaded his fingers carefully through her hair, not disturbing the knot at the back. "I like your hair better this way," he said musingly, and she felt the heat from his body. Only centimeters between them, her breath shallow and painful in her lungs. "Gives a man something to dream about," he murmured. "Freeing all that golden wildness."

His eyes were on her hair, but his fingers slid down to her throat, hesitated at her collar. Her breath was turning jagged, raspy in her throat. She tried to control it, failed, her eyes wide, staring up at him.

"Your body remembers me," he said softly. "Doesn't it?" Abruptly, he moved away. "We'll start again, shall we?"

"Start . . ." Her heart was crashing against her ribs, heavy blows of panic, or longing. "Start what?"

He shrugged. "Parenting. We have a daughter. It would be crazy for us to be strangers."

She whispered, "What are we, then? Friends?"

He smiled. "Why not, Abigail? After all, you're a modern woman, aren't you? It's nothing, these days, being friends with an old lover."

An old lover.

She had seen him across that crowded room, had recognized all those things in him. Safety, security...
home. Of course it had been wrong. Some illusion. Or
a crazy illness, a virus she had succumbed to from shock
and lack of sleep. It could not happen again. Insane,
how that made her tremble, just remembering his hand,
hers accepting, nestling in his grip.

He knew. He came closer. His hands dropped to her
shoulders. She sucked in a gulp of air. He pushed gently,
turning her to face the wall. His fingers touched her back,
caressed lightly up until they were on her head, her hair.
Undoing the clasp. The hairs at the base of her neck
pulled painfully for a brief instant, then the clasp was
free and she could feel her hair falling wild through his
fingers. She felt him threading his fingers through,
spreading the strands out, around her shoulders. She
could see the scattered confusion of her own hair trailing
over her shoulders and down toward her breasts. Her
breath came in painful gulps.

He cupped her shoulders in his hands, catching hair
and fabric and Abby herself, pulling her back against
him. Hard. Warm. She tried to hold herself away, but
she could feel her body sinking into his maleness.

His breath teased the hair near her ear. "Your body
remembers," he said, his voice low and magnetic.

She turned. Or he turned her. She did not know which
it was. She stared up at him, his eyelids drooped over
shades of brown-and-gold. His lips were a straight line,
parted slightly. She knew the kiss was coming. His lips
moving to hers, his hands threading through her hair,
making it a wild softness against her neck, her cheeks.
His mouth taking hers in a caress from dreams.

"No!" She jerked and there was nowhere to go. She
gasped, "Friends, you said. Not this!"

Then she was free.

"I'll claim you one day," he promised quietly.

She could hear those words long after the echo of his car had faded away. She dreamed him. His arms around her body. His mouth against hers, whispering lovers' promises that turned her blood to fire. In the dream she opened to him, wild and hungry and needful, begging him to possess her.

She woke in the night, heated with passion, the darkness all around and the memory of his touch on her. He had haunted her for so long. The old memory. "I'll claim you one day."

He would hold his hand out and she could walk with him wherever he led. She would be lost then, because it had not been loving in his eyes. She had trusted herself to a stranger once, had married Ben with dreams and fantasies in her heart. This was worse, far more risky. God knew what it was pulsing in her blood, but she dared not lose herself or she could be living her life on the edge of disaster, aching for his voice on the telephone, for his knock on the door. Forever.

The next week, Abby talked to Hans about Trish's aversion to her art classes, and he amazingly agreed that it might be best to let Trish cancel her extra classes for the time being. As for Ryan, he seemed to have forgotten his original harsh demand that Hans get out of Trish's life.

Abby had never intended to push her daughter into a life of art, but somehow it had happened. Hans's pressure mainly, she supposed, but she herself was to blame for not seeing how uncomfortable it all made Trish. As for Ryan, she seldom saw him alone. He turned up on Friday evenings with Trish in his car. His picking her up from school had become a ritual they both accepted. He was around each Saturday and Sunday, going back to his hotel each night. He had changed hotels, moving into nearby Duncan.

At first Abby was nervous, watching Ryan and Trish, but slowly she relaxed. They were lazy weekends, filled with idle conversation, walks to the beach, dinners out in town and sometimes they all went to the theater. Ryan's camera was always there, inconspicuous but active, and he promised to give Abby some good pictures of Trish for Christmas. When Sunday afternoon came, Ryan always drove Trish back to school.

If it were not for Trish, she thought he would be gone. He spent most of his weekdays away somewhere. He mentioned New York once, and she knew his publishers were there. One week he flew to London to visit his sister, and sometimes she suspected he flew down to his cottage in Mexico. He seemed to fly to the other end of the world with casual regularity, but all through the rest of October and November he returned without fail to pick up Trish from school each Friday.

Everyone she knew seemed to have decided that Abby and Ryan were having a flaming affair. Her mother kept dropping his name into the conversation, while Sandra offered to stand in for Abby any time she decided she needed a break from all that masculine magnetism.

"And those eyes," breathed Sandra. "I would die for those eyes."

Abby gave up protesting. No one believed they were only friends. Everyone thought they were lovers—or about to become lovers—but the truth was that they hardly saw each other without Trish present. He telephoned her once a week, on Thursday nights.

"Abby? I'll pick up Trish tomorrow from school."

"All right," she would agree.

"Anything you need from town?" he would ask, and she had begun keeping a short list for him. Milk. An extra loaf of bread. Some fresh fruit. It was a strange intimacy, his bringing a bag of groceries as if he were coming home from work at night, calling first to see what she needed.

As if they were a family, which they certainly were not.

"Are you going to marry him?" asked Trish early in December. Ryan had just left, promising to return the next day and take them both down to Victoria for a Christmas shopping trip.

"No!" denied Abby, her voice too loud, too abrupt. "No," she repeated, and it sounded more convincing the second time. Dreams, she thought miserably. She had to stop reaching for impossible dreams.

Trish shrugged and said with studied casualness, "I don't mind, if you want to. He's okay."

"We're just friends," said Abby, but Trish did not believe that any more than Sarah had. Ironic, that everyone thought they were lovers, even Trish who was the reason he came. Abby said, "He comes to see you," which was the closest she had come to the truth for all her resolutions to tell everyone the truth, to get the threat out of her life.

Except that there did not seem to be a threat now. Just Ryan, staying close, making himself part of Trish's life. Part of Abby's life, too, although that was probably not his intention. "I'll claim you," he had said, but he had hardly touched her since then and Abby was pretty sure now that he had not meant it.

Trish frowned and said thoughtfully, "You're getting older, you know, Mom. I'll grow up and get married and you shouldn't just live alone."

Abby choked back a laugh at her daughter's relegation of all adults as imminent victims of senility, but she could not help feeling even more conscious of Ryan that weekend. Damn Trish! She was going to have to tell her daughter the truth eventually, but she did not know how she could explain it. And what if Trish was upset? All her life she had believed Benedict Stakeman was her father, although of course she'd never known him.

The weekend dragged and Abby avoided Ryan's eyes, because he might see the question in hers. Did he remember telling her that he would claim her one day?

He had not meant that. Of course he hadn't. It was only anger, and when he was ready to start another book he would be gone. Off to Africa or South America or China, leaving his trail in pictures that left people breathless from exposure to the heart and soul of a strange, faraway culture.

But first there would be Christmas in Mexico, where Ryan had a cottage on the beach. As the weeks passed, Trish became more and more excited, questioning Ryan endlessly, although he never seemed to lose patience.

"What about your passports?" Ryan had asked Abby back in November.

"They're up-to-date," she told him. "Trish and I often go on holidays with Mom and Damian. Will we need a visa?"

"Not for Mexico. We'll get tourist permits at the airport in La Paz."

She had smiled, thinking of ten warm winter days with Ryan and Trish. Mexico, and it felt to her as if she would be flying into a dream place where there was no need to worry about anything at all.

They left from Vancouver International airport four days before Christmas, flying first class to Los Angeles, where they changed to an Aeromexicana jet for the flight to La Paz. Trish sat between Ryan and Abby. To Abby, it seemed that her daughter asked questions nonstop until an hour before their landing in La Paz. Then Trish fell asleep abruptly, her head resting on Ryan's shoulder.

"She's run-down," said Ryan with a quiet laugh.

"I don't wonder." Abby's smile answered his. "She's been thinking of nothing else for weeks." She turned to look through the window beside her at the dramatic desert mountains ten thousand meters below their plane.

His hand reached across their daughter to possess hers. "What about you?"

"Yes," she admitted, turning back to smile at him. "I've been looking forward to this holiday, too. But she's better prepared than I am, you know. She's been studying Spanish on some tapes she got from her French teacher. All I know is *buenos dias* and *gracias*."

Ryan said, "I'll look after you," and she felt a warm happiness growing inside, as if he meant it forever.

He woke Trish as they were circling over the harbor city of La Paz, telling Abby, "We'd better give her a few minutes to get over the growlies, hadn't we?"

Abby put her hand on Trish's arm as the girl grumbled to wakefulness. She always woke with a grumble, but Ryan's mentioning it made them seem a family. Abby felt an odd sensation, as if their both touching Trish in the same instant were Ryan's touch on her own flesh. She told herself it was dangerous to feel this way, but his eyes were on hers and she felt a sudden, breathless intimacy.

Outside the La Paz airport terminal, the sun was high and warm.

"Hot," said Abby, shrugging off her woolen suit jacket.

Ryan chucked. "Ask the locals, they'll tell you La Paz is cold in the winter—Trish, here! The car's over here."

It was Ryan's car, one he had explained to Abby earlier that he kept in Mexico. "Rental cars in this part of the world are pretty chancy. You might get a twenty-year-old *bomba*, so I bought my own to keep here.''

The drivers, she discovered, were insane, but Ryan handled the traffic smoothly, and after a few minutes Abby relaxed. There might be a bunch of maniacs on the road, but he would get them through safely.

''Just a different style of driving down here,'' he told her with a smile.

''Are you a mind reader?'' Ahead of them, an old red truck swayed down the road with a crablike motion.

Ryan said, ''If I were, this would be a lot simpler.'' He signaled and made a turn, then they were out of the city, heading up into the hills.

''What would be simpler?''

''How far?'' demanded Trish. ''How far to your place, Ryan?''

''An hour's drive,'' he told her patiently for the seventh time that day, but he did not answer Abby's question.

Simpler? What did he mean? Abby watched Ryan throw Trish an affectionate glance. That was it, of course. He was her father, and it was only natural he wanted Trish to know. He had promised that he would not tell Trish without Abby's agreement. But he intended to persuade Abby in time that it was best if Trish knew the truth.

Being able to read her mind would help in that. Abby frowned, knowing she had hoped he meant something else, had hoped he might want a lasting relationship with her. With every hour they spent together, he became more a part of her life. Each day, it became harder for Abby to imagine a life without Ryan close by.

The highway between La Paz and Ryan's beach house led through sun-dried hills and cattle ranches. Twice Ryan had to stop for cows on the road, once for a group of Mexican cowboys crossing on horseback, an event Trish found exciting enough to take her mind off the endless hour to Ryan's place.

"I'm putting that in my report," Trish announced, scrambling for her notebook. "When I get back, I'm giving a report to my Social Studies class on Mexico, and the cowboys are ace! Ryan, what do you call cowboys in Spanish?"

"Vaqueros," he told her.

"What do the cows eat?" wondered Abby. "This seems far too barren for rangeland."

Ryan said, "I know. Amazing, isn't it, that cattle can make it in these mountains? They eat cacti, among other things. It gets less arid up ahead. Todos Santos is quite green."

Just before they came to the town of Todos Santos, they drove through a lush abundance of palm trees, then the village with a policeman standing on the edge of the highway, a visible deterrent to speeding through the little village. The policeman waved to Ryan.

"A friend?" Abby asked.

Ryan nodded. "I gave him a ride to La Paz once."

"A hitchhiking policeman?" It was a far cry from home, and she said slowly, "Is that what you do when you go into a country with your camera? Learn the language and the people and immerse yourself?"

"More or less. Although, when I was in Iraq I had the devil of a time with the language."

She realized that she was watching the flow of expressions on his face. He seemed relaxed today, his face easier to read. "How many languages do you speak?"

He shrugged. "Six or seven with fluency. The rest I just know pidgin stuff. I can pick up the Romance languages fast enough—Spanish and French and Italian—but I have a miserable time with Arab dialects."

She shook her head. "I can't even imagine how you do it. I barely passed French in school, and I live in a country where all the labels are in French and English." Trish must have inherited his ease with languages. She loved French classes and already seemed to have a lot of Spanish, just from those three tapes her teacher had lent her.

Ryan said, "It's just a knack. I grew up with foreign languages all around. That probably made it easier. I could teach you French if you want."

She shook her head, knowing that when he went to the next place, for the next book, she would miss him terribly. She stared out of the window at the colorful taco stand they were passing, then the sandy dunes that led toward the beach. He was not a man who would stay. He would come back, of course, for Trish, but if Abby reached for him in the end she would be alone with the memories.

His beach house was alone in a stand of palm trees, facing toward the open Pacific ocean, with slow waves coming in from the sea. It was one story, larger than she had expected, with a palm-leaf roof.

"It's called a *palapa*," he explained. "The palm leaves keep it cool inside. The Mexicans often have roofs purely of dried palm leaves—you'll see it in restaurants quite often. This has a wooden roof, though, with the *palapa* over for coolness."

Inside, the house was simply decorated. A ceramic tile floor with braided rugs, Mexican carvings and a bright Mexican blanket on the walls. Ryan led Trish to a small bedroom with a door directly onto the patio. It was, thought Abby, very much a young girl's room. There was an elaborately dressed Mexican doll sitting on the dresser, a bright embroidered spread on the bed. Trish went to the doll first, touching the folds of the dress, whispering, "Some day I'll have a dress like that. When I'm grown up, I'll get married in a dress like that."

"She's yours," said Ryan. "Make yourself at home."

"You came down here to get that room ready for her, didn't you?" asked Abby as Ryan led her down the corridor to her room.

"Yes." He glanced back at her with a smile. "It was my storeroom, actually. Books and odds and ends."

"When?" She wondered which of the flying trips he had made had been here, to prepare his Mexican hideaway for his daughter.

"A couple of weeks ago."

Ryan opened another door and Abby touched his arm before she stepped past him. "That was nice of you."

He looked down at her with an inscrutable expression in his eyes. "I can be nice sometimes," he said finally, and she felt her lips curving into a smile. "Your room," he said, nodding.

She moved into the large bedroom. It was all quiet and warmth, a wall of windows bringing the ocean close. She moved slowly across the braided rug, circling the big bed, pulling the wardrobe door open.

Men's clothes inside, pushed to one side. The other side empty, for hers.

"This is your room?" She turned back and he was still in the doorway, his eyes narrowed as if he were thinking of taking a picture.

"I'm sleeping in the darkroom," he said mildly.

"Oh." She felt her heart start to beat again as her face flushed. "I—I couldn't—with Trish here, I—couldn't." It was, she realized, an admission that she *would* share his bed if he asked at another time.

"I know that, Abigail." He crossed the room and placed her suitcase on the bed.

She moved toward the case, toward Ryan. When she stopped beside him, he turned and took her face in his hands, stroking gently with his thumbs. She slid her arms up around his neck, threading her fingers through his hair. She had just admitted that he could ask and she would be his. Now she needed his warmth. For a moment there was stillness, breathless quiet as their eyes spoke. Then his mouth came down to hers, and she stretched up to meet his lips.

Soft. Gentle. His lips probing hers, tongues touching, exploring slowly. Then the fire began to burn and the kiss turned deeper and shattering, driving a sound from deep in his throat and an answer from her heart. His hands slid down her back, bringing her close as she strained closer, sending the heavy pulse beating deep inside her, her softness seeking his hardness.

A door slammed somewhere.

Suddenly it was gone, Ryan's arms dropping away from Abby. She stepped back, or he did. She tried to look away, but could not, could not breathe, could see her own need, her own desire, reflected in his eyes.

She heard footsteps, coming closer. She said unsteadily, "Trish."

"Yes." His hand fell to her suitcase and she realized then that he had started to reach for her again, had stopped himself when she spoke their daughter's name. "Another time," he promised. "Soon." He blinked and she saw a mask go over his face, hiding the desire that had been there only a moment ago. "I'll go to Trish. You unpack, lie down for a while if you want. It's been a long trip."

Then he turned and went out into the corridor.

Abby could hear his voice, and Trish's. Her daughter was talking about a walk on the beach and Ryan was telling her never to go into the water without either himself or her mother right there. Trish promised solemnly that she wouldn't, then Ryan said something Abby could not quite hear and Trish laughed with happiness.

Ryan would be her lover. Soon, he had said, and she could no longer pretend that she did not yearn for this man with her whole being. They would be lovers, and when he left for the next book she would have new memories to hold close.

CHAPTER SEVEN

CHRISTMAS at Todos Santos with Ryan was ten days of pure magic.

On Christmas Eve, Ryan took them out to a restaurant to celebrate Trish's birthday. While they were eating the *enchiladas* that Trish had immediately fallen in love with, a group of musicians came to circle the table and serenade an overwhelmed Trish.

"You'll have to come here for your fifteenth birthday," Ryan told her afterward with a smile. "When a girl turns fifteen in Mexico, it's a big celebration. She's serenaded outside her bedroom window."

"Wow," breathed Trish. "Wait till I tell the kids about this!" She had taken pictures of the musicians with the camera Ryan had given her as a birthday present, and Ryan had promised to develop them for her in his darkroom before they went back to Canada.

Abby had looked thoughtful when Trish opened the present earlier, wondering if this was a way for Ryan to say that Trish was *his* daughter.

"She wanted one," he had said mildly, correctly interpreting her expression. Then, as Trish went to get ready to go out for their celebration dinner, he had added, "I intend to see that she has the chance to grow up to be her own person."

In some ways, he had already done that. Before Ryan came into her life, Trish had always been a little too serious, too intense. Now she laughed more, and Abby often heard her voice raised in excitement.

On Christmas morning, Ryan gave Abby an album of pictures of Trish. He also gave her a case for her sketching materials that folded into a portable easel. The case was filled with the best quality pastels and an assortment of charcoal pencils.

She understood that this gift had a message. He was telling her, again, that he believed she was talented, that she should take her own art seriously. She had not known what gift to choose for Ryan, but had settled finally on a framed sketch she had done of an old derelict boat. It was one he had particularly admired, and when he opened it he came across to give her a slow, deep kiss.

"Thank you, Abby," he said softly. "There's only one thing you could have given me that I'd have appreciated more."

"What?" she asked, but he only smiled and she felt herself flushing.

Then Trish said, "You guys better get married if you're gonna spend all your time kissing," and Abby jerked away, pushing the wrapping paper into an empty box and managing to avoid Ryan's eyes until enough time had passed for Trish's remark to have faded.

But it was her dream, too, that Ryan would love her and want to be with her forever.

The next day, she started sketching Ryan's beach house with the *palapa* roof that made it look so thoroughly Mexican. Ryan dug out something he called a boogey board and, with the slow swell rolling into the beach, began to teach Trish to ride the waves on the board. Then he came up the beach and took Abby's hand, laughing when she resisted.

"Your turn," he said. "You'll enjoy it."

He was right. She felt free and wild riding the waves on the board. When he caught her just as a big swell swept over them, she went into his arms willingly, clinging as his lips took her deeply, quickly, into passion. As the water tumbled over them, he held her tightly to prevent her being swept away.

There were only a few days, but they slipped into an easy magic. Trish spent most of her time on the beach, making firm friends with a Mexican boy who came to fish off the rocks with a hand line. Ryan spent part of each morning in his well-equipped darkroom, developing the pictures that he took as automatically as breathing. Afternoons were for lazing in the shade, early evenings for lazy walks along the beach. Abby found herself using the new sketching materials each morning, looking at her own work with a critical eye and wondering if Ryan could be right. This was what she loved. She always had, but Ben had persuaded her that she had no talent and she had believed him.

Ben himself had been a talented artist, but he would not have wanted his wife to compete in any way. Abby had known that from shortly after their marriage, but had believed that her own lack of talent was one of the reasons he had chosen to marry her.

"I like that," said Ryan when she finished the picture of the beach house. He had been sitting in a beach chair, watching her work with a quiet interest that oddly did not make Abby nervous.

Abby felt warmth at his praise, realizing that Ryan was confident enough of his own talent that he could praise others without feeling threatened himself.

They flew back the day before Trish's classes started again, stretching the holiday out to the last minute. When they got to Canadian Customs in Vancouver, Abby realized that she'd completely forgotten about needing to declare the gifts they were bringing back. It was Ryan who had thought of it all ahead, producing receipts and a list of items and getting them through Customs smoothly.

"I'm the accountant," she said uneasily afterward. "I should have thought of it."

He said, "I told you I'd look after everything," but she could not help feeling nervous at the way she so easily forgot the rest of the world when she was with Ryan.

Ryan delivered Trish to school, then Abby to her home in Maple Bay. "I won't come in," he told her as he helped her out of his Porsche. "I have some business to clear up, but I'll be back in a few days."

"All right," she agreed, avoiding his eyes. Only a few days ago, she had as much as promised to become his lover. Now she felt awkward and nervous. It would be insanity, because she would give too much, would need too much from him.

Then he would leave.

The next Monday, Abby started north on her rounds. She did the farmer north of Duncan first, then on to the fisherman. By Tuesday afternoon she had worked her way up to the little garage at Campbell River, and she worked there through the afternoon until the staff were ready to lock up.

Dark fell early in January. It was black outside when she finished. She was only a few meters away from her van, but she did not see the man until he spoke.

"Hello, Abigail."

She stopped, frozen.

"Ryan," she breathed. Her voice was faint. She could see her breath, frost on the air.

Ryan was wearing his bomber jacket, his hands pushed into the pockets in deference to the January chill. The white glinted in his dark hair like frost lying there. She clenched her fist to stop herself reaching to touch him, to feel that he was real and not one of the fantasies that had haunted her waking hours since he dropped her off at her house the other day.

"Nice to know you can say my name now without going into shock." He almost smiled. "Can I take you to dinner?"

"All right," she agreed. "Of course."

He took her out to Quadra Island across the harbor, a ferry ride that seemed to pass quickly in the quietness of his car. "Have you got this on permanent rental?" she asked, running her hands along the seat beside her thigh.

"More or less," he agreed, his eyes amused. "I like comfortable cars."

"Comfortable?" She laughed. "This isn't *comfortable*, it's decadent." All around them were cars and trucks crowded onto the little ferry. The vehicles were a strange mixture. Several of what the locals termed "island cars," battered but still running. A couple of shining new trucks. One small red city car. And Ryan's Porsche.

He was smiling as he said, "A little decadence is good for the soul."

She thought of the places where he went to take his pictures and thought perhaps she understood. "Where are we going for dinner?"

"A lodge on the other side of Quadra Island. Good food. Quiet. Which hotel do you stay at up here?"

"I sleep in my van."

He frowned. "I don't like that. Do you at least go to a campground?"

"This time of year?" She laughed. "They're all closed."

"This time of year," he echoed grimly, "you must freeze."

She shrugged. "I've got an Arctic sleeping bag, and a catalytic heater. And I've been doing it for years. Don't fuss."

The lines in his face deepened harshly. Was he going to demand she use motels in future? If he did, they would have a battle, because of course he had a right to be in Trish's life, but he had no rights over Abby. And if they became lovers . . . if they—well, he'd still have no right to tell her what to do. She sat beside him in silence, trying to work up anger and resentment, failing because he had not given her cause yet.

They had not touched. When she came out to her van and found him waiting for her, she had thought he had come to make his promise good. Soon, he had said. And she had been waiting.

Waiting for him to make her his.

That was not why he had come, she decided now, because he had not touched her, had not kissed her hello. His eyes now were cool as he glanced at her. She had to be demented to yearn for a man who could look at her as if she were a stranger, as if she were something caught in his camera viewfinder.

They were going to a quiet place, he said, and she supposed that after they had been served dinner he would tell her why he had come. Something to do with Trish, perhaps. When he brought it up, she would tell him that she had decided to tell Trish the truth.

He drove off the ferry and along the tree-lined road in silence. Abby watched the trees and the half-hidden houses go by, feeling oddly content, knowing she was falling under his spell as she always did. When he parked in a small space among the trees, she opened her door and swung her legs out, stood up feeling disoriented with trees and water and old, dark buildings all around.

Ryan took her elbow as they moved away from the car. "This way," he murmured, leading her toward a massive wooden door that opened onto a quiet lantern-lit dining room.

The smiling hostess greeted Ryan by name and smiled at Abby. "Dinner for two?" she asked.

Ryan's hands settled on Abby's shoulders as she started unbuttoning her coat. When he slid the coat away from her, he said softly, "Very nice."

She was wearing a peach sweater that buttoned down the front, a soft scarf tucked in at the neck, and a swinging wool skirt that echoed the sweater in darker tones. A nice outfit, but nothing unusual, although she flushed at his words and the dark lights that sprung into his eyes.

"You've been here before?" she asked when the waitress had settled them at a table in a shadowed corner of the room.

"Yes. I've been staying here for a couple of days."

Staying. She picked up the napkin at her place, pleated it with her fingers. "Taking pictures?"

"A few," he agreed.

"What you spend in film in a month would keep me in clothes for years."

His lips twitched. "That's an exaggeration, but perhaps not by much."

"You said you had business to attend to?"

"In Vancouver," he agreed. "I came up here Monday."

She studied the menu for so long that Ryan said, "Shall I order for you?"

"Yes," she agreed, although she hated other people making up her menu. Ben had always done that, and she had let him because she was young and he had seemed to want to take control that way.

She was seated with her back to a wall covered with ancient, faded navigation charts of Vancouver Island. Behind Ryan, she could see shadowed impressions of old photographs on the far wall. It all seemed hazy, except for Ryan across from her, his harsh face and disturbing gaze. She kept trying to look away from him, but her eyes were pulled back, and she watched him turn to give the waitress a brief smile as he ordered for them both.

A shadowy man slipped into the far corner of the dining room and began strumming low and moody on a guitar while Abby sipped on the wine Ryan had ordered for her. He must have noticed which wine she drank at home. And he had ordered oysters for her dinner. She loved oysters, although she thought there was no way he could know that. She supposed he knew her preferences the same way he knew everything. He was a very observant man, perhaps part of his training as a photographer. She avoided his eyes and pretended they were not watching her and perhaps they weren't, because she managed to relax with the low music from the guitarist.

Outside, a broad expanse of shadowed lawn led down to the water where there was a small marina lit by overhead lights. It all looked empty and unused, the summer sailors long gone back to their fireplaces for the winter.

Abby said musingly, "I'd have thought all these tourist places out on the islands would be closed this time of year."

"Most are," he agreed.

"You talk as if you know them all." She could not help smiling.

He shook his head. "I've been around, though. Taking pictures."

"Pictures for you? Or for someone else?"

"Your ministry of tourism. Larry decided that since I seem to have settled here for the time being I should be put to work. I sometimes wonder how he finds these things."

Larry was his New York agent, and Abby knew that the men were also close friends. Sometimes she thought that she had actually met the people in his life. Larry, who negotiated the contracts with publishers for Ryan's books and stored some of his personal possessions. Emma, his sister, who lived in London and looked like Trish. Ryan had looked after Emma when his parents died, and she still called him when she had problems. She was twenty-eight and just separated from the husband Ryan disliked, and Ryan worried about her.

Abby even felt sometimes that she knew his parents, the quiet, humorous diplomat and his wife who had died in an earthquake when Ryan was eighteen. She stared into her glass and tried to push back the questions on the edge of her mind.

Where do you go when I don't see you? What do you do? Are there women? When will you leave for the next book?

She lifted her glass.

Much of the dining room was lying in shadows. Over dinner, Ryan told her about the photographs he had been taking, while Abby told him about her attempt to help Dennis track down the thief on his staff.

"Dance?" he asked when the waitress had cleared their dinner plates.

"No, I—I should get back." His arms, holding her, drawing her near. "I left my van at the garage."

"It'll be safe there, I would think." He set his glass down and stood up. She could read nothing in his face. His eyes were in shadow.

She felt her fingers clenching in on themselves. He held out his hand to her, waiting. She rose stiffly, avoiding his hand, walking ahead of him to the small area that had been cleared for dancing. Alone. Just the guitarist strumming moody rhythm, and Ryan turning to hold out his arms to her. She moved awkwardly to place her hand on his shoulder, her arm stiff to keep a distance between them.

"Relax," he murmured in her ear. "The world won't end if you lie in my arms."

It might, she thought, and her tension made their movements awkward across the hardwood dance floor. She had been with him for only a few hours in London, an intimacy that had surpassed everything else in her life. He had been in her dreams ever since that afternoon. It had felt right and easy to move into his arms in Todos Santos where she knew Trish's chaperonage kept her safe, but now she was aware of just how shattering it would be if he became her lover, of how easily he could hurt her.

He took the hand that rested in his and placed it on his other shoulder. They were standing, swaying, facing each other with no more than a breath between them. One of his hands slid up her back and found the fastener in her hair.

"Don't," she breathed, but it was too late. Her hair was sliding free. His fingers were threading up into her scalp. He was going to kiss her, here on the dance floor. She could feel his fingers in her hair as it flowed free. She swallowed a lump of panic and anticipation, knew that if he took her mouth with his she would be lost.

She should not have had the wine. It had gone to her brain, slowing down her reactions, leaving her too long in his arms, panicked and uncertain if she could free herself. She pulled back, thought wildly that perhaps she should have had more of the wine, not none. She stepped back farther, fighting a need to go forward and let her arms find their place around his neck.

"Watch out," he warned. He caught her arm. She twisted and he pulled her against him to prevent her stumbling into one of the empty dining tables.

"I've had about enough of this!" he muttered impatiently.

Back at their table, she picked up her bag, avoiding his gaze, making the kind of motions that should tell him the evening was over. She'd had enough, too. If he wanted to see Trish, they would have to find another way. As for Christmas—ten days living under the same roof as Ryan, watching him moving around in shorts and bare chest, dressed for the warmth of the Mexican winter. It had seemed inevitable in Mexico that they would be together, but this was her home, her country, and he was a foreigner who would leave soon.

He left her. To pay the bill, she supposed. Then he was back, holding her coat. When he turned her to face him, she pulled back and fastened her own buttons awkwardly.

"In a hurry?" he asked with quiet harshness.

"Yes," she agreed, focusing on the buttons. "Let's go."

Then, abruptly, they were outside, cool January air on her face and darkness around. There were traces of a brief snowfall under the trees at the edge of the lawn, but other than that the place was green dying into a mild coastal winter, salt air and clouds gone dark with night above them.

He said, "You should come up here and sketch this place," and she stared at him because earlier she had been thinking much the same thing. Except that she would never come. The trees and the water would be tangled with Ryan, the man with the dark hair and the eyes that she sometimes thought she could see through.

"You should do an exhibit," he said abruptly.

"We did one in September." She was relieved to talk about ordinary things. She said mechanically, "All Ben's paintings are gone except for the few in the house. I kept them for Trish. Did you pay our bill? In the dining room?"

He turned away from the parking lot, drew her along the shadowed edge of the buildings. "You kept the paintings for Trish?" he demanded, leaning back against the corner of a small, dark cabin.

She flushed in the darkness, realizing what she had said.

His voice was so harsh that she knew his eyes would be dark with tightly leashed anger. "Did you really pretend all these years that she was not my child? Inside yourself, did you?"

She turned and could see only his dark silhouette against the trees. "I tried to," she said quietly. "What else could I have done? Everyone knew. Ben announced that I was pregnant to the whole world at that showing. We had thought I was, you see, and I'd found out it was a false alarm, and...it was hard, telling him. I never did manage to tell him. There wasn't time, and I hadn't the nerve."

"The nerve," he echoed. "He would have been angry?"

"He'd counted on it, and when he told everyone—— They all knew, so when I had a baby—what could I do? They thought they knew the truth, and it seemed best to just..." Abby shrugged helplessly.

He said quietly, "You could have come to me."

"You were a stranger." Her heart crashed louder with each beat in the long silence that followed her words.

"Was I?" he asked finally, his breath white in the air between them.

He was going to move closer, or reach out and pull her against him. She hugged herself tightly through her coat, gasped, "Give me my barrette. For my hair." He handed it to her and she bent her head, caught her hair and fastened it, needing to make a barrier somehow and knowing this would never be enough. No, he had not been a stranger. A part of her had ached to find him when she learned that she was carrying his child.

He murmured, "You should wear combs. Ivory combs, antique and fragile."

She shook her head, felt a hair caught in the clasp of the barrette pulling painfully.

"About that exhibition you should have, I didn't mean an exhibition of Stakeman's work, Abigail. I meant yours."

"I'm not that good." Did he know that she had dreamed of his arms around her all these years? Secret yearning, needs she could not acknowledge even to herself. She shook her head wildly, said on a rush, "My *work*, as you call it, is just——"

"Stop it!" His hands locked on her shoulders, shocking her into silence. "So help me, Gail, if you call your sketches *doodles* once more, I'll shake you until you..."

His lips were covering hers. She felt the trembling deep inside herself. His hands slid down her arms and curled around her fists. She felt her body straining against her will, desire moving toward him. His lips, his kiss, and she would drown in him.

The kiss was brief and light, a mere teasing caress of her mouth. She felt her own lips swollen, parted in invitation. She almost cried out when he drew back.

"Don't call me Gail," she whispered desperately.

His fingers released her hands, moved to trace the shape of her cheeks, her jaw, her throat. His voice was husky with the night. "It was Gail who gave herself to me."

She let her breath out in jerky stages. He had a key in his hand, was fitting it into the door of the small cabin. "I'll claim you one day," he had said, and now he pushed the door open and turned to wait for her.

She gulped and could not move.

"Are you coming in?"

She pushed her hands into her coat pockets, hunched her shoulders and walked through the door. She heard it close behind her, did not turn to look. A light went on, low and dim, near the door. It was a three-room cabin, living room here, kitchen and bedroom beyond. She was standing near the sofa, staring at a fireplace where the coals had burned down to a dull red glow.

He walked past her, shedding his jacket, moving to the fire. She watched him laying new logs on the coals, and when he finally turned to look up at her, his eyes were quiet and shattering.

She shook her head mutely. They both knew she could turn and walk out of the door. There would be some way to get a taxi away from this seductive, quiet place, and he would not stop her. They both knew she would not go.

"You're afraid." His voice was abrupt. "Why?"

So many reasons. No reason.

"I'll protect you," he said. "There won't be a baby this time."

She bit her lip to stop the trembling. He must be doing this deliberately, torturing her. They both knew this would end in the next room, in that bed. She was his, had always been his. If he cared to claim her, he could have her. At some level, he had understood that from the beginning.

But *he* belonged to no one, and she thought she had always known that, too. Now, watching him as he crouched by the fire, she admitted to herself that even in the darkness of her grief and confusion back in London, she had recognized Ryan in her heart. She would have recognized him any time, in any place.

He rose silently from the fireside. "I said I would protect you."

"I'm on the Pill," she blurted.

"Since when?"

Would he leave her nothing? Could he somehow see through her to the center even without light? "Since...a couple of months ago."

He knew there had been no one else. All those years, and she had held herself alone and safe from loving. He moved slowly and when he began to undo the buttons of her coat she could hardly feel his touch.

"Ryan..."

He slid the coat from her shoulders, turned and hung it in the small closet. "Pick out some music," he suggested. "I'll get us something to drink."

She crossed the room, crouched down beside the table filled with compact discs. She reached out and saw her own hands steady, wondered how that could be. She took out a disc and put it in the portable player she recognized from Mexico. His player. The lodge where he was staying.

He had been waiting for her at the van, had known she would be there in Campbell River and had come to...to... 'I'll claim you," he had said, and all evening, while she was trying to keep herself safe, he had known how the night would end.

She heard his soft footfall on the carpet, jerked and dropped the plastic disc case. He put two glasses down on a low coffee table in front of an overstuffed sofa, then bent down and picked up the case. She focused on the drinks. Hers looked like the same wine again, which was almost the only thing she ever drank, and he must have bought some, stocked the kitchen.

"Sit down," he said, gesturing to the sofa. "You must know you needn't be afraid of me, Abigail."

She felt as if he had turned on an overhead light instead of the soft glow near the door. She hated waiting, knowing he must see how vulnerable she was to him.

He said, "I want to bring Lyndon Boydon over to look at your work."

She sat abruptly, edging into the corner of the sofa. "Is that what you were doing in Vancouver?"

"Partly." He did not sit down. He picked up his drink and took it to the fireplace, said rather grimly, "You should be doing something with those drawings. Limited print editions, I would think, but it's not my line of country. Boydon will know."

"No," she said then, finding her voice at last. "I don't want——"

"Why does it bother you so much? What harm to let Boydon have a look?"

She said desperately, "Could you sit down? Stop looming over me. It makes me nervous."

He laughed and muttered something about everything making her nervous, but he sat down in the middle of the sofa, so that she could not move without her legs coming up against his. She studied her hands and admitted, "He might say they were interesting—my sketches. But he'd only want to make capital out of the fact that I was Ben's wife."

"What did he tell you about your work?"

"You mean Ben?" He nodded, looking grim, and she almost laughed. "Not much. Just that I had a knack, that it wouldn't do any harm for me to play around, but not to expect it to come to anything."

"Doodles?" he suggested.

"Yes," she agreed.

He was angry, which surprised her, then his gaze narrowed and he said, "He was a damned fool! Either that, or he knew just what kind of talent you had, and deliberately suppressed it, which would be criminal."

"Please don't say anything about my sketches to Lyndon Boydon. Not yet." He did not answer, and she realized then that neither of them had pushed the buttons to start the music playing. Silence, the crackling of fire in the fireplace. He took her hand in both of his and she felt the sensations running over her skin, through her bloodstream.

"Are you always afraid to take chances?" he asked gently.

She swallowed. Chances like loving this man. "Yes," she said. "I guess I am a coward. I always was."

"I'll help you," he promised, then, "Turn around," he said in a voice gone low and husky. "I want to take that thing out of your hair."

She turned her head away from him, sitting up straighter, feeling his thigh brush against hers. She glanced down and saw her skirt lying across his leg. Then she felt his hands at the back of her head and a sigh escaped. He freed her hair and his fingers played through the long softness.

"I love your hair," he murmured. "Winter colors in your hair now. I've watched it change all autumn." Her neck lost its strength as he bent to press his lips against her throat. "Golden hair everywhere," he murmured.

"Dark and light. I remember how it lay on my pillow, your eyes closed, your face so tender and . . . I must have photographed every long-haired blonde in the world."

"I know," she breathed, felt her head falling back against the sofa.

"None of them was you. You haunted me." He slid her glasses off and put them somewhere.

Her eyes opened, stared up at the harshness of his face. He had dreamed of her. She asked on a whisper, "What is it that you really want from me?"

No answer, just his lips against her eyelids, his fingers flowing through her hair. His mouth brushed hers, parting it on a sigh and taking the sweetness waiting there for him. His fingers tangled in the softness of her scarf and she felt it sliding away. Then the backs of his knuckles grazed down along the opening at the neck of her sweater and the breath left her lungs with a harsh sound that he took from her mouth.

"Yes . . ." she whispered, the sound falling on her ears as a stranger's. Of their own will, her fingers tangled in his hair where it waved against the back of his neck. His hand found her thigh through the skirt, then he was lifting her, shifting her to lie with her skirt strewn across his legs, leaned back against his arm with his dark head blocking out what light there was.

His eyes, lids drooping over them, watching underneath as his fingers slowly freed the buttons of her sweater. Her breath turned ragged as he pushed the knitted fabric away. A whimper escaped her throat as his fingers brushed across the lacy fabric of her bra.

She twisted, her arms snaking around his shoulders, pulling herself against him, her lips against his. She felt the shock go through his body as she pressed close. She moved her lips restlessly on his until he took charge of the kiss, plundering deeply as he drank from her mouth.

Spinning, dizzy, she lost track of touch and sensation, just the whirling vortex of his arms, his mouth taking hers in shuddering symbolism of the ultimate surrender of woman to man.

He pushed her back against the sofa. Her hands went restless on his chest, fingers finding their way through the buttons of his silk shirt, spreading out through the tight mat of his chest hair. A sound escaped his throat and she pushed his shirt away, her lips and teeth seeking against the heated roughness she found there.

"Abigail..." He swept her up into his arms so that she lay captive against him, her skirt and hair sweeping down from his embrace. The firelight lit his eyes and she could see the iron grip of control he still held on himself. She reached up with her arms, brought his lips to hers so that she could surrender, felt the crush of her soft breasts against his hard maleness.

He carried her somewhere, lowered her to softness. "You're a witch," he growled. If she was, she thought, then she would make *him* lose control. He freed her bra, then he bent to kiss the soft swelling of her breasts and it was too late for her to take control of anything. Her fingers slid through the crisp waves of his hair, gripping desperately as he tortured her with soft caresses of his tongue on her nipples. When he drew her inside his mouth, she heard the sound and knew only in its echo that it was she who had cried out.

His thigh moved to part her legs and she was tangled in him, holding him close, hearing his whispers without knowing the words, making noises herself that might have been begging or just sounds only a lover could know.

"Yes," he murmured, "yes," and she felt her hands slide over his naked chest, gripping his shoulders as he moved to possess her. She heard herself cry out as she moved to him, as he entered her the way he had in dreams.

In her restless dreams he had been tender and gentle. She had moved to him quietly, taking the comfort he gave. Here, now, he was moving in her, taking her mouth in deep possession that left her crying for more. Her head was thrashing restlessly, moving in growing wildness against the softness of the mattress as he drove her beyond sanity, beyond bearing.

She heard the scream echoing through the darkness, sought desperately in his arms, his possession. Then the wild desperation turned to blazing purpose, harder, closer, pulsing within them until she felt his cry and heard her own self exploding in a trembling tumult that sent her spinning through the universe... until she clung sheltered in his arms, his lips against her breast silently telling her forever...

CHAPTER EIGHT

RYAN said, "I think we should get married next week."

Abby froze, feeling the motion of the brush through her hair.

She had woken alone, her face and her body flushed with the echo of intimacy. Instinctively, she had reached for the first thing she could find to cover herself. His shirt, hanging on the knob of the headboard. His brush, lying on the bureau. She had taken it and sat on the bed, brushing her hair, breathing slowly and deeply, drawing in the lingering scent of Ryan from his shirt, listening to his sounds from the next room. The kitchen, she supposed, because she could smell coffee. When she heard him coming closer, the soft pulse of his bare feet on the floor, she had bent her head forward and brushed the hair down and down, over her face. Hiding from him.

She had felt him close, her body growing sultry and lethargic from the knowledge that he would touch her. Then his hand had taken the brush from her nerveless fingers and he had moved behind her. Kneeling on the bed, brushing her hair, stroking through its length. Incredible that her body could go heavy and pulsing just from a brush moving through her long hair... from the knowledge that he was behind her, that his caresses could send her mindless and desperate.

That was when he told her they should get married.

"Why?" she demanded, surprised that her voice sounded so strong and aggressive. "Why do you think we should get married?" She reached back and swept her hair to one side, over her shoulder where it fell across her breast. Then she turned and took the brush out of his hand before she met his eyes. They were all colors, brown and green and gold. Every color and no color at all.

"Trish," he said quietly. "That's one good reason."

Love would be another, but he had never said he loved her.

Abby stood up. She walked over to the bureau in her bare feet and put the brush down very carefully, quietly. Then she walked into the kitchen and the pot of coffee was there. Of course it was Trish he really wanted. She got a cup down and poured for herself, and she could hear him behind her, coming into the room.

"Do I get a cup?"

She reached up for another cup. "Is Trish the only reason?"

He said, "We're compatible, you and I," and she could hear the shrug in his voice, but she did not turn to look. She poured the second cup of coffee and he added, "And you're obviously not involved with anyone else."

"Obviously?" She turned to face him, her face carefully blank.

"Last night. I could hardly help knowing it had been a long time since you'd been with a man."

She knew that her face was flaming, but she kept her expression carefully blank. His gaze dropped to the hem of his shirt. The shirt covered her to mid-thigh. Below that, her legs were long and bare. He might be remembering any one of a dozen moments. Perhaps that instant when his hand had brushed against her center, the way her body had melted and cried out for him.

She swallowed twice and then said steadily, "It's not enough."

His eyes went dark. "When you marry me, I could adopt Trish."

She turned and picked up her coffee, moved to the table and sat down, lifting the cup and sipping, knowing he was watching and he must know what she was feeling. When. Not if. There was probably nothing he could ask that she could refuse. She loved him, and it was going to hurt for a long time, because he wanted her daughter and he wanted her body, but nobody had mentioned anything about love. She did not dare say the word. Passion, and, while she might go wild in his arms, it would never be enough when dawn came.

"Yes," she said. "All right."

She had laid her own trap almost twelve years ago. There was no escape now. She got up and took her coffee with her as she went into the bedroom. Last night ... but this morning he had not touched her. Just her hair, brushing it, but no kiss, no tender smile. No words whispered in her ear, lovers' words that surely should be said when morning came.

What did *she* know of lovers? She was a fool. A bloody fool. She closed the bedroom door and he was on the other side of it somewhere. She dressed hurriedly, could not find her barrette anywhere, left her hair loose. She rammed her glasses on her face and opened the door and he was sitting in the living room staring at the fire.

"I've got to get to work," she announced.

"I'll drive you," he said, as if she were someone he had met casually. A stranger. He had never felt like a stranger to her, even at that first glance, and she was not hiding behind dreams any longer. She had known him then, knew him now. He could reach down to her soul with a mere glance, but, although he had once said she haunted him, he'd had her now and it was only dust in his eyes, an obsession that could not hold his heart.

He helped her into her coat, put on his own jacket and held the door for her to leave. He turned on the radio in the car when they got in and they drove without conversation through the tree-lined island, listening to a mixture of news and music all the way to the ferry.

Perhaps he was planning his next series of photos, or thinking of the last. His camera was in the back seat, but last night he had taken no pictures. She shuddered, because he had taken pictures in London, his voice warm and reassuring through the whir of his camera. She looked out the window and hid behind the blond curtain of her hair. When he delivered her to her van, she opened the door before he could do it for her.

"Abigail?"

She turned back, her hands shoved deep in her pockets, her hair a curtain between them.

"We'll go down to get the marriage license on Friday."

"There's a waiting period," she said flatly.

"Yes, I know. We'll plan on a week Saturday."

She unlocked her van and went into the back where the computer was. She sat and watched the blank screen and finally she heard the Porsche moving away. Then she went to the driver's seat and watched through the window until the gray car was only a memory.

"You're late this morning," said Dennis when she came in.

"My timing's off today," she told him.

She left Dennis at noon. By that time they were fairly sure they knew who the pilfering employee was. Dennis was going to set a trap for the culprit, while Abby went on to the next client. By Thursday noon she was finished and on her way back home.

She stopped the van when she passed an abandoned log house, got out her sketchbook and sat in the open sliding door of the van trying to get a feeling for who might once have lived in this cabin, who might have worked and sweated to build it as a place to come home to.

When she was done, she looked at the sketch and it made her feel warm and melancholy at once. Perhaps she *should* let Ryan bring Lyndon Boydon. Perhaps she could bury herself in her drawings. She had seen an artist in Victoria, selling prints in one of the shopping centers. Limited editions. Ryan had made it sound very professional, but what if she tried and failed?

She drove home, arguing with herself, wondering if Boydon could be trusted to give her an unbiased opinion of her work. The telephone was ringing when she came through the door to her house. She dashed toward the kitchen extension, got there in time to hear the dialing tone. She grimaced and dropped the receiver into its cradle. Upstairs, she found that she had forgotten to turn on her answering machine when she left on Monday morning.

She was loading the data from her trip into the computer when the phone rang again. "Hello?" she said, and her voice was breathless before she heard his answer.

He said abruptly, "I'll pick you up at eleven tomorrow."

"Pick me up?" She had been expecting him to tell her he would pick Trish up from school, and for a moment she felt confused, disoriented. Then she remembered. The marriage license.

"You'll be ready?"

What if she said no?

He said, "We'll collect Trish afterward, perhaps go out to the theater." It was not really a question, so she made no comment.

Her mother called next, asking, "How was your trip north? Was it cold up there?"

"Not very." Hot and disastrous, she thought, knowing that she would walk into the same inferno again if he held out his arms.

"And dull?" asked her mother, laughing at Abby's tone of voice.

"No," said Abby. "Not dull."

"You and Damian," Sarah complained. "How can you get pleasure out of a computer and a bunch of numbers? By the way, Trish phoned me while you were away."

"Was everything okay?"

Sarah laughed. "She can call her grandmother without an emergency, can't she?"

"Of course. But I've been wondering lately if she's really happy at school."

She would talk to Trish. If the girl did not want to be an artist, surely there was no need for her to be away at a special school every week. She could go to the intermediate school in Duncan, take the school bus. Abby frowned, because she had no idea whether Trish liked the school, and she *should* know. Did Ryan know? Trish was so withdrawn in some ways, holding her thoughts behind those green eyes. Like her father, thought Abby, and knew that this time she could not let herself be swept along by circumstances.

Sarah was saying something about Christmas. Abby said, "Yes, it was wonderful."

"She's so excited," said Sarah. "Full of talk about cowboys and surfing on some crazy little foam board, and a Mexican boy she met. And...what on earth is going on between you and Ryan Marsdon anyway?" Sarah laughed at her own question. "I can guess just *what* is going on, but...well..."

"I don't know," said Abby. She supposed she could have said they were getting a wedding license tomorrow, but, even if they got the license, the wedding would never come to pass. She had to do something before then, but she was not at all sure she wanted to talk about it, even to Sarah.

"Figure it out before it's too late," warned Sarah, "That's a man you could regret letting get away. And Trish likes him, too, which you must realize is a lucky stroke. Some people haven't got it so easy. Second marriages and children can be like oil and water."

The trouble was, it was too easy to close her eyes and picture Ryan in her bed when she woke... Ryan rising early to make her coffee while she was still tumbled with sleep... Ryan across the table... Ryan calling home to ask if she needed him to bring anything home... Ryan reaching to bury his fingers in her hair and draw her close and...

But, even married, he would leave her. She had dreamed of going with him when he did the next book, and it was easy enough to dream, but the reality had none of the loving warmth her fantasies were laced with, and a wedding license would not make him want her with him when he went traveling.

Sarah was saying, "Haven't you seen the way the man looks at you? He's not playing games, you know. And you need a husband."

"I've managed for years without. I don't need anyone." It was a lie, but Ryan would never give her what she really needed. Words of love on his lips, vulnerability in his eyes. He was a man who had never been vulnerable to anyone. Passion and desire, perhaps, but not love.

"You've been lonely for years," said her mother. "No man's been able to get near you. And ever since Trish went off to school, I've seen you becoming more and more alone. You need a man like Ryan, someone to love."

Abby shook her head, caught her flyaway hair with her free hand and made herself say the words. "He's her father."

"Well, you can't expect that..." Her mother's voice faded to silence abruptly, then she demanded breathlessly, "What did you say?"

Abby closed her eyes and formed the words slowly. "Ryan is Trish's father." Silence. "He—I met Ryan in London just after Ben died." Abby closed her eyes and felt the trembling slowly steady while her mother took in the shock.

Sarah said, "But everyone knew you were expecting Ben's child."

Abby shook her head, although her mother could not see. "I thought I was pregnant, but I wasn't, only I hadn't gotten up the nerve to tell Ben because he seemed so set on it. And—well, he announced it to everyone in London. So everyone knew. But it wasn't true."

"You met Ryan...the baby wasn't late at all?"

"No."

Abby closed her eyes and remembered the hospital, the impact when the baby was placed in her arms. When Abby had looked at her baby, she had seen Ryan Marsdon looking back at her.

"Does he know?" breathed Sarah.

Abby twisted the coils of the telephone cord around her finger. "Trish is the image of his younger sister. Green eyes and all." She choked laughter back, knowing it was hysteria. "So, you see, it's not a romance at all. He's hanging around for Trish, and I can't get married to make tidy parents for my daughter, can I?"

Had she told Ryan that she loved him? She might have said anything back there in that cabin on Quadra Island. She knew that he had not made any vows of love to her. Lovers' caresses, yes, and he loved her hair, the curve of her hip, the soft seductive swelling of her breast under his lips. Lord knew how many women he had said that sort of thing to, passion and warmth, but "I love you, Abigail" was not part of what he was offering.

When Sarah hung up, Abby went downstairs and started getting her supper ready. Sarah would tell Damian, and Abby was sure she could count on her stepfather not to react badly. Two down, she thought, her mother and stepfather. Hans. Well, she was not looking forward to telling him, but she thought he would accept the truth once he got over the shock. It would not change his love for Trish.

The problem was, how was Trish going to react? Abby could not begin to guess her daughter's reaction. Trish liked Ryan, had been blunt in saying she would accept him as a stepfather. But finding out that he was her real father...?

Trish next, she thought, not Hans. When Abby told Hans, he might do anything. He would be hurt at first, and angry. He had a right to that, and when she did tell him she would have to make sure he did not have a chance to see Trish until he'd had time to cool down.

She was ready when Ryan came the next morning. She had dressed carefully in a long denim skirt and a soft blue sweater. A farce, getting this license, but she could not face that issue until she had faced the other. "The truth shall make you free." She buttoned her coat when she heard his car and went out to meet him. He was just getting out of the car as she closed the door. He watched her walking toward him, one hand on the roof of his car, the other loosely clenched into a fist at his side.

"You look nice," he said quietly.

"Thank you," she replied politely.

She moved to the passenger side of the car, but he got there before her. He bent down to tuck in her skirt and coat before he closed the door. She realized that he was not going to touch her, just the hem of her coat, and her breath slowly released.

He went around to the driver's side. She watched him passing in front of the car through the windshield. He looked handsome and unyielding, not a man in love, but a man who had made a decision and was determined to carry it out. She locked her fingers together as he got into the driver's seat and looked forward through the windshield.

He said, "They've got Big Bird wandering around at the shopping center near my hotel. Would Trish like to visit Big Bird, do you think?"

Abby tried to laugh. "She might be insulted if we suggested it. Kids' stuff, you see." *We.* She bit her lip and made her voice bright and superficial. "I suggested Santa Claus last year and she informed me she'd known there was no Santa for years. Apparently she sneaked out of bed one Christmas Eve and saw me putting the presents under the tree."

He turned off the gravel road and onto the paved secondary highway that would take them to Duncan. "I'd like to have known her then."

She had been wrong to keep the secret all those years. A man had a right to know he had a child, and Abby had stolen those years from him, because he plainly loved Trish now that he knew her. She had never thought of his wanting children. She had assumed that he was too busy traveling the world, taking pictures instead of living life. He kept himself separate with that camera, looking at the world through a lens.

But when he'd seen Trish . . . when he'd realized . . .

"Were you ever married?" she asked abruptly.

"No."

She gave the button on her coat another twist. "Why not?"

She had not intended to turn and look at him, but somehow her eyes went to his face. It told her nothing. He was driving, concentrating on the winding road. He shrugged and she saw his shoulders shift in the suit jacket he was wearing. She preferred him in casual clothes, the bomber jacket and blue denim jeans, his shirt cuffs rolled back and the hair on his forearms showing. Today, his whole outfit—tie and jacket, immaculate gray trousers—turned his eyes impenetrable.

She said, "Back in London you told me that you didn't want chains. Is that why?"

"No." He pulled up at a traffic light and asked, "Will you have your stepfather give you away?"

She could not marry him like this, as the price for being Trish's father. Compatible, he said, but it would be better for them to have an affair than to tie knots around each other, setting themselves up for disaster when he decided he no longer wanted her, when she could no longer bear to live close to a man she would love more each day.

Waiting for the traffic light, he turned to study her. "Have you told your mother?"

She shook her head.

He released the brake and the car surged forward. "You'd better tell her tonight. Give her some warning."

She said stiffly, "You mean, in case Mother and Damian have something else on next Saturday?"

"Yes, that's what I mean. I assume you want to be married in a church?"

Her fingers clenched together. "Why would you assume that?"

Watching her. Always watching, picking up bits of knowledge without his heart being in them. If he loved her, he would surely have held his arms out when she came across the drive from her front door, not opened the door and tucked her in as formally as if he were the chauffeur and she the madam.

Now he said, "I don't see you pledging your troth in a register office. Where do you prefer? Duncan or Victoria?"

"Victoria," she said mechanically. "From my mother's."

Once Trish knew Ryan was her father—well, they would have to make some arrangement about visiting. People who were divorced did it, and that must be even more difficult, dealing as strangers with a man you had once lived with.

He said, "We'll fly to Mexico after the wedding. Unless there's somewhere you'd rather go for our honeymoon?"

Todos Santos. Just her and Ryan, sharing that big bed that looked out onto the beach. She shuddered, hugging herself in the passenger seat, watching him turn and glance over his shoulder as he began to park the car outside the courthouse.

As they came out of the courthouse, Abby saw Ryan tuck away the piece of paper that was their marriage license. Two days, the clerk had said. Two days and the license would be valid, but Abby did not have two days. Ryan obviously intended to tell Trish about the wedding when they picked the girl up from school. Somehow she had to stop that.

"Lunch?" suggested Ryan.

"Yes." She would tell him over lunch.

He turned and drove south, away from the town, pulling up finally at a large log structure. Inside, everything seemed bright and cheerful, the waitress showing them to a table in the corner. Abby stared at the chinked logs rising up into the second storey of the building, the balcony above them. Ryan obviously had an affinity for log buildings. The lodge on Quadra Island had been log as well. Logs in Canada, a *palapa* in Mexico.

The waitress tried to take Abby's coat, but Abby held on to it.

"I feel chilly today," she explained.

"Coffee?" the waitress asked.

"Yes, please," said Ryan, and Abby nodded. There was a menu in front of her and she studied it carefully.

The waitress returned with coffee and announced the special. Abby nodded and Ryan said, "I'll have the special as well, thanks," and they were left alone again, only now there was no menu to stare at.

Ryan reached across and moved her cup to one side before he took her wrist in a firm grip. She felt the strength of his grip. His eyes were flat, emotionless.

"You haven't said a word since we left the courthouse." His mouth looked harsh, the lines on either side carved deeply into his face. His eyes were narrowed, watching her, and she supposed he must have realized that she was not going to play her part in his plans.

"I can't marry you."

His fingers on her wrist tightened, but nothing at all happened in his face or his eyes, unless the lines grew deeper.

She said nervously, "It's not—I can't—you can't just get married without being in love. It doesn't work." She looked down at her hand, caught in his grip. Her hand was pale and thin under his broad, dark fingers. She could see the black hair growing across the back of his hand. She could feel the heat from his grip, and determination. She wanted to beg him to love her, to hold her and never let her free. Which was exactly why she must *not* marry him.

"Love, Abigail?" His voice was grim. If there had been any hope in her heart, it died then.

"Yes," she whispered. "I—you—I'll tell Trish the truth." She glanced up quickly and saw a muscle jerk in his jaw.

"Tell her what truth?"

"That you're her father."

He leaned back and picked up his coffee, still keeping her hand imprisoned. "How are you going to explain that?"

She bit her lip. "I don't know. I'll—the truth, I guess."

"Did you love your husband when you married him?"

"Yes," she said, because it was true as far as it went. There had never been the shattering impact Ryan had always had for her, but she had thought she loved Ben, a pale shadow of the emotion that raged through her life now. She said, "I thought I did, at least, but I'm not sure he loved me." She had never said that to anyone, hardly even to herself, but now she said with quiet conviction, "And there's no way I could let myself get into another marriage unless it was for love. So I'm—sorry, but we'll just have to work out about Trish and...and it'll work out somehow without—without..." She shrugged helplessly.

The waitress appeared and set a plate of steaming ham in front of Abby. She felt nausea well up. He was saying something about Mexico and she shuddered, but whatever happened she was not going to cry.

He let go of her wrist and said, "Eat your lunch," as if there were nothing more at stake here than a good lunch. She picked up her fork and stabbed it into the ham steak as he said, "Then we'll go and pick up Trish."

"Ryan, didn't you hear me?" Her voice came out squeaky and it was no wonder he looked surprised.

"Yes," he said tonelessly, "You don't want to marry me." He shrugged and for once his eyes did not meet hers. "We can work it out. There's no need to get in a panic over it. Meanwhile there's the weekend, and we'll pick up Trish——"

"No!" She dropped her fork and the man sitting at the next table turned to look at her with his mouth parted in startled protest. She whispered harshly, "*You* pick up Trish. Or *I* will. But *not together*. I'll talk to her. This weekend. I'll—— And you can see her, of course, but not—not at my house. You can—can pick her up and take her out. We can ... come to some——"

"Arrangement?" he suggested, his voice soft like a whip, and every bit as harsh. "Visitation rights?"

"Yes," she agreed, her hands gripped around her cup. He *was* furious.

"At least you told me this time. Going on your past performance, I'd have expected you to leave me waiting for you at the altar. Just as I waited for you in London."

She shivered and whispered, "I—I—it doesn't really matter to you, does it? You didn't need me then, not really. You just—and now—it's Trish you want, isn't it? You don't need *me*."

He shrugged and there was no need for him to answer in words. She managed to push her chair back and say clearly, "I'll—I'll go back for my van and pick up Trish. You—you could call Sunday and ... I'll have told her by then."

"I'll drive you."

She said, "No" sharply, in panic. "There's a bus. And I—I don't want you. Stay and ... eat your lunch." She turned away quickly, before he could see the lie in her eyes. She grabbed her coat, almost upsetting the chair. Then she moved quickly, away from Ryan, past the other diners, the startled waitress, and through the door.

CHAPTER NINE

ABBY locked her van and stepped onto the pavement that wound through the immaculate grass outside Allison House. All afternoon the words had been going around in her mind. Around in circles, over and over. She would tell Trish the truth. It was past time.

Ryan is your father. I love him and...

He's gone.

He could come on Sunday.

No, he would not. She did not know what she had expected from him when she told him they could not marry, but it had not been anger. Silly, because he certainly had a right to anger. She had acted like a fool. Saying yes, meaning no. Wanting him to love her and afraid to say so because he didn't.

A woman's voice called across the lawn, "Mrs. Stakeman!"

Abby did not hear. She pushed her hands into her coat pockets as a gust of wind whipped around her coat. Typical coastal winter. No snow, just wind-driven chill penetrating to the bone. She bit her lip and knew he would not come. She would have to tell Trish the truth anyway. Too many lies.

"Mrs. Stakeman! Hold on!"

The raised voice finally penetrated and she turned, hunching her shoulders against the wind. It was the principal's secretary, running, coming to a panting stop in front of Abby. "Mrs. Stakeman. I've been calling and calling. Mr. Donnell wants to see you in his office."

Abby frowned and followed the secretary toward the administration building that towered over Allison House. The secretary was dressed in only a skirt and sweater, running for cover. Abby followed more slowly, head bowed against the cold. When she pulled open the heavy door to the office building, the secretary had already disappeared inside. Abby could hear a telephone ringing somewhere.

Mr. Donnell met her in the foyer, guided her into his office with a hand on her elbow. He was frowning, so it must be something serious. Perhaps Trish had actually failed something. A failed test would be grounds for ex· ecution in this place. She stuffed her hands more deeply into her coat and hoped she was not going to lose her temper. She rarely gave way to anger, but today it would be easy. Emotions were a storm boiling just below the surface of her skin.

"Sit down," he instructed, but before she could manage that he was muttering, "We have been trying to contact you all day. Your answering machine, Mrs. Stakeman, is not particularly useful when what we need is consultation with a parent. And may I remind you that it is one of the requirements at Callman that an *alternative* number be given, another relative or mature friend who can *reliably* be contacted."

"You've got my mother's number. What——?"

"*Reliably*, I said. When we tried to call this afternoon after the accident, there was no answer."

"Accident?" She stood up, focused on him and repeated, "What accident? Where's Trish?"

"Patricia is at the regional hospital. She was taken there by ambulance an hour ago."

Abby turned and found the secretary standing behind her. Donnell's voice was saying, "Ms. Clathers will drive you to the hospital."

Abby demanded in a high, brittle voice, "What happened?" She jerked back to look for his answer, saw his lips parting.

Time, minutes ticking past. Trish in the hospital.

Afterward, Abby could not remember driving to the hospital. Just the instant when she jerked the van to a noisy halt outside the hospital emergency entrance. Then, inside, she got lost in a confusion of voices, white uniforms and placating words.

She heard her own voice raised, screaming, "I want to see my daughter!" Then she swallowed and gulped on the lump and whispered to the middle-aged woman in front of her, "I'm Abigail Stakeman, and my daughter was brought in earlier by ambulance and *please*, can you find out where she is and—and if she's okay?

Please don't let her die.

It echoed in her mind, chanting, driving her mad as she paced the empty waiting room. It seemed forever, then someone led her to a room, and behing the white screens she saw Trish, pale and lifeless in a sea of white.

Abby moved toward the bed. "Oh, no! Is she... Trish?"

A man dressed in white intercepted her. "She's barely conscious. You can stay for a moment, very quietly, then I'll talk to you outside."

"Our family doctor——"

"I've spoken to him." He nodded his head, indicating they would talk outside.

She touched Trish's hand and found it cool, almost cold. She whispered, "Trish? Honey?"

Trish's eyes fluttered faintly, but did not open. Abby whispered, "Mommy's here, Trish," then the nurse touched her arm and Abby followed the doctor out into the corridor.

He led her into a small office, closed the door. "Your daughter's had a serious fall. There appears to be some internal bleeding in her cranium. The indications are that there is pressure building——"

"Her head? Indications? What does that mean?"

He said quietly, "Her pulse . . . pupils . . . respiration. The fact that she was conscious when she arrived here, but is now losing consciousness. We've had her under observation all along, of course."

"Observation?" Pressure inside her head. It sounded the sort of thing horror stories were made of. Abby whispered, "Can't you . . . do something?"

"In these cases, all we can do is observe until there's some sign of damage." He must have used this quiet voice to thousands of relatives. "In the last half hour, there have been indications of pressure. Your family doctor and I have agreed that she should be sent down to Victoria where she can be under the care of a neurologist."

"Victoria." She realized that she seemed to be repeating everything he said. "Can I—how will she go?"

"By ambulance. Dr. Carridine will be waiting for your daughter in Victoria. You can travel down with her in the ambulance if you wish."

"Yes." Her hands clenched on her handbag. "Do I— is there some kind of consent I have to give?"

"The nurse will take you down to administration. They have the forms. We've been trying to reach you ever since your daughter was admitted, of course, but in the absence of a consenting guardian your family doctor and I have signed consent for her emergency removal to Victoria. In an emergency——"

"Yes," she agreed. Her voice sounded impossibly normal. "How will I know when the ambulance comes? Can I be with Trish until then?"

She felt oddly rational and in control, but she must have been fooling herself because she lost track then.

Forms and strange faces, white uniforms and someone she had never seen before telling her not to worry. Then she was at a telephone, fumbling for a phone book that was not there, calling directory assistance for the number of Ryan's hotel, dropping the quarter twice before she got it into the slot to make the call. A woman answered after three rings and told her cheerfully, "Sorry, Mr. Marsdon checked out earlier this afternoon."

Abby felt a sick recognition that was not surprise. Gone. Of course he was gone. "Could you——?" She gripped the receiver and felt pain in her fingers. "Do you know where he can be reached?"

"Sorry," was the cheerful reply, "I'm afraid I can't help you."

"It's urgent."

Trish, lying motionless in a room down that corridor. Unconscious now, the nurse had said, but they would not let Abby in to see her until the ambulance arrived, which was supposed to be any minute now.

Abby closed her eyes and said in a stiff voice, "His daughter's had an accident. She's been sent down to Victoria by ambulance. If he—if he calls——?"

Suddenly, the voice became human. "We do have a 'care of' forwarding address and telephone number for him. I'm afraid it's not much help, because he didn't sound as if he planned to go there right away."

It was a New York address. Abby recognized the name. Ryan's agent. She had to fumble for her calling card to make the long distance call, then a deep, well-modulated voice in her ear identified itself as Lawrence Willman. She was instructed to leave a message at the sound of the beep.

Her fingers clenched on the receiver. "This is Abby Stakeman. If—if there's any way you can get hold of Ryan Marsdon, could you tell him his daughter's been hurt?" She gave details hurriedly. She could see someone who looked like a doctor walking down the corridor.

When she hung up, the man wearing the white lab coat walked past her with his gaze on something at the end of the corridor. Abby went back to the waiting room, but Mr. Donnell was there now, pacing, assuring her in a nervous voice that everything would be fine.

"What happened? How did she get hurt?"

"It was lunchtime." He frowned deeply. "And she should have been in the cafeteria, but she was playing on the roof of Allison House." His brows lowered and he said sternly, "Students are *forbidden* access to the roofs. Patricia knows that. All our students know the rules."

She turned away and went to the window, looking out at a parking area, cars coming and going, a woman in an unwieldy cast maneuvering her way along the walk. Then she heard what she thought was a siren and she spun around and the nurse was there.

"Mrs. Stakeman? The ambulance is here. If you'll come now...?"

There must have been an ambulance in London, herself and Ben transported somehow to hospital. Abby could not remember, must have been knocked out herself for a while. She was glad now that she had missed that part, because doing it now was terrifying, sitting inside the back of the vehicle as it screamed along the roads with siren going. Then they were out of the city, turning and driving up the Malahat highway over the mountain to Victoria. Trish was lying with an intravenous needle in her arm and her black hair tumbled all around her face, her eyes closed as if they would never open again.

Playing on the roof during lunch hour? That did not sound like Trish at all. She was more likely to watch the others breaking rules, her green eyes narrowed. Abby hugged herself tightly as a surge of pain swept up. She needed Ryan. Here, holding her in his arms and telling her it would be all right. Even if he went away afterward, right now she could not . . . hated hospitals and waiting and . . . ambulances.

Eventually, they came to Victoria. Lights and the doors swung open at the back so that the ambulance attendants could slide Trish out. They took Trish away, left Abby with papers and forms to be signed.

Later, she found herself in a quiet waiting room somewhere upstairs. She had arrived by elevator, someone in a white uniform at her side. She was alone now, staring at the doorway, until a thin, gray-haired man dressed in a quiet suit came to her.

"Mrs. Stakeman? I'm Dr. Carridine, the staff neurosurgeon."

"Surgeon?"

He smiled gently. "We have your daughter under observation. She's stable at the moment, but you do know that she's unconscious?"

Abby nodded and the surgeon explained that Trish had pressure building up inside her skull, an indication of bleeding inside. "Often these things heal themselves, so we wait and watch. If the pressure increases, she might need burr holes."

"Holes?" Her voice had a brittle, horrified sound. "Holes in her skull?"

"Yes," Dr. Carridine said. "It's not a drastic procedure, and it may not be necessary. We won't know for three or four more hours."

"Can I see her?"

"For only a moment," he said gently. Then, he suggested, it would be best if she went to a nearby motel and checked in, had a rest. She shook her head. There was no way she could leave.

Finally, after brief seconds with a pale, unconscious Trish, Abby ended up in the same place she had been in London when Ben died. Waiting in a cold, sterile room filled with uncomfortable chairs. Trish might never wake up again. Abby felt the tears and willed them back, her eyes burning, dry and open wide. Alone again, waiting.

Then the nurse.

"Mrs. Stakeman, why don't you go down to the cafeteria? Have something to eat. You really should go away and rest, you know. Is there someone we can call for you?"

She shook her head, went herself to the pay phone and called her mother. No answer, of course. Mother and Damian had planned to go to Vancouver this weekend. Abby had no idea what hotel they might have chosen to stay in. She thought of trying to call hundreds of hotels, starting at the beginning of the alphabet and working her way through them all. Then she realized there was no Vancouver telephone book here anyway, and directory assistance was not likely to cooperate in giving her the number of every hotel in a city the size of Vancouver.

She went back to the waiting room and watched the second hand circling the big clock on the wall. How long? Ryan would be in Mexico by now, if that was where he had gone. She was positive he had gone to Mexico, but she had no idea how to reach him when he got there. There was no telephone in the beach house. She gripped her eyes tightly closed, knowing she must not let herself even think that Trish could lose this battle.

What if her thoughts made a difference?

She got coffee from a machine, forced the liquid down because it would keep her alert and she needed to stay absolutely in control. She watched the second hand pass the six. It was dark outside now. Winter nights. Trish, eyes closed on light and life.

The nurse came and again suggested Abby go to the cafeteria for a sandwich. She shook her head, thinking of lunch. Ryan, his angry eyes burning into her. He must hate her, because of course he had wanted more than visiting rights. He had wanted to make a home with his daughter, and...and Abby should have tried to give him that. She suspected that he did not easily put his feelings into words, would have found it hard to explain to her how badly he wanted Trish to live with him. He talked with his camera, his eyes. Maybe... Oh, God! She must not cry!

She stood up and her empty coffee cup fell unheeded to the floor. She went to the window, but there was nothing there. She paced back to the doorway, but the corridor was empty except for a nurse pushing a trolley. Back to the window.

Sit down! she screamed silently at herself, but she could not. She could not cry, must stay in control. Trish had to be all right.

A man's voice murmured her name. "Mrs. Stakeman?"

Abby turned, her hands behind her, gripping the windowsill. The neurosurgeon was standing in the doorway. He looked tired. Abby tried to read his face, to see the truth behind the noncommittal words, but there were only words.

"...take her into surgery...relieve the pressure..."

Part of Abby wanted to scream, demand to *know*, but of course there were no answers. Waiting, and the answers meant nothing at all.

Then Ryan came through the door and at first she thought she had dreamed him. Tall and lean and big in a gray wool overcoat. His gaze swept the room, stopped when he found her. She moved toward him and he crossed the room and took her hand and she clung to his, cool from the outside air. Then he was questioning the surgeon and the surgeon was frowning, demanding to know who he was.

"Her father," said Ryan, and when the surgeon's eyes sought hers she nodded. She felt dizzy, but it was as if Ryan's presence had touched her, holding her up. Without him, she thought she would have sagged to the floor in a pool of helpless fear.

He turned and pulled Abby into his arms and she buried her face in his chest, the tweedy fabric of his overcoat against her face "It can't happen again," she mumbled into his chest. "I hate hospitals."

He lifted her chin and stared into her eyes. Her glasses were smeared from rubbing against his overcoat, or perhaps she had let some tears escape. He said, "I know, honey. How long have you been here?"

Hours. Forever. Ryan took her glasses off and slipped them into his pocket. Then she was sitting down and he was beside her, holding her hand tightly with his. It seemed forever, but she was clinging to his hand, and it was just under an hour before Dr. Carridine came back.

He was dressed in green, cotton booties over his shoes and a mask hanging around his neck. "Yes?" said Ryan, and he was motionless, waiting for the answer.

Abby kept her eyes closed. Coward, she screamed at herself. She heard the words though.

"...still unconscious...surgery fine. No complications...pressure relieved...wait and see...next twenty-four to forty-eight hours critical...see her for a minute, but then best to go and get some sleep yourself."

Then Ryan was holding her hand, and carrying on holding it when they saw Trish, her head swaddled and her face so pale. She was all fuzzy, but Abby did not ask Ryan to give back her glasses. She was afraid to see more clearly. Only a second, and they were ushered back out of the room, then Ryan was leading her away.

"Tell me what happened," he demanded quietly, and she realized that he was trying to make her talk, wondering if it was for the information, or just to help her keep her balance.

She said tonelessly, "They say she was playing on the roof of her residence. She fell. It doesn't make sense. It's not the kind of thing Trish would do. She doesn't like heights."

She wanted to touch his face, to be back in his arms. She wanted to cry and knew that she must not do that. She stopped dead in the middle of the corridor and Ryan said, "Come on, Abigail."

"Where? I can't——"

He drew her against his side and put his arm around her, holding her close and supporting her at the same time. "It's right next door. The motel across the street, and we'll tell the nurse at the nursing station."

"Trish might need me." He turned her to face him, bent and placed a kiss on her motionless lips. She wanted to tell him not to do that, because if he kissed her, she would start to feel again. Instead, she said flatly, "I can't leave Trish."

"The surgeon says she's unlikely to wake before dawn. They won't let anyone see her until then. And if she should wake earlier, we can be here in three minutes."

Wake, he said, as if that was all they were waiting for. Trish to wake.

Then they were in the elevator, going down. Then through the doors, walking out into the cool night air. Abby stopped suddenly, feeling things slipping out of her control. "Trish," she said, panicked. "I can't—I've got to stay with her."

"We'll be right here." He pointed to the building looming across the street. "Only a minute away, and I'll call to check on her every hour." The quietness of his voice emphasized the near hysteria in hers. She felt a sudden urge to scream at him for being so calm. She bit her lip and he led her across the street, the streetlights glowing with soft coronas because she could not see properly.

Inside the motel room Ryan booked, Abby's eyes flew to the telephone. Ryan glanced at her, then walked past her into the washroom. She heard water running.

"I'm running you a hot bath," he told her when he came back. "You're shivering, and you're too damned tense." He crossed the room and she thought he was going to take her into his arms again, but he took her shoulders in his hands and looked down at her, frowning. "It's going to be all right, Abigail. I promise you."

"Am I supposed to take your word for it?" She shuddered.

"Yes." She knew that was impossible, but oddly his conviction comforted her. He said, "Now go in and soak in that tub."

He pushed her toward the bathroom, but the telephone rang and Abby froze, staring at it in horror. Not until morning, the surgeon had said. She would not wake for hours. If they were calling now——

Ryan had picked it up, listened for a second and said quietly to Abby, "It's okay. It's just the desk..." He spoke into the receiver. "Yes, that's right. We'll let you know tomorrow."

Abby realized that her teeth were dug into her lower lip. "Was that——? Why did they call?"

He slipped open the buttons of his suit jacket. He was dressed very formally, as if he were trying to be a stranger to her. He said, "The night clerk hadn't asked how long we were staying. Nothing important."

She shivered, feeling the cold crawling deeper, and thought she would never be warm again, that hot baths could not soothe the horrible tension inside her. He glanced toward the bathroom and she said, "All right, I'm going," stiffly, and turned and walked away from him.

She closed the door behind her and started pulling off her sweater. Then her skirt, which fastened with a long series of buttons down the front. It fell in a heap around her feet and she stood in bra and panty hose, staring at her own reflection in the mirror, thinking that she looked strange. Fuzzy, too, because he still had her glasses.

Ryan called quietly to her, "Don't lock the door."

She had not locked it. "Why not?" she asked, thinking it was stupid to make words that did not matter when Trish was in the hospital. She closed her eyes and thought she could see her daughter. Those bandages around her head. They must have shaved her head. Trish would hate that.

"Abby? Are you all right?"

She saw the doorknob turn and then Ryan was standing there, staring at her. She stared back and even without her glasses he looked harsh and strained. She said, "Are you afraid I'll pass out in the tub?"

"Just don't lock it," he said in an odd voice.

"Ryan, do you think they've shaved her head?" Her voice cracked.

If he put his arms around her she thought she would start to cry, but he didn't. He came to her and turned her around, then he unfastened the clasp of her bra and slipped it off. Then he bent to slowly strip her panty hose off and she felt nothing.

"Would they have shaved her head?" she asked again.

The panty hose was down around her ankles. He was kneeling in front of her. He placed her hand on his shoulder and said, "Lift your foot," and slipped the nylons off her right foot. "Now the other one," he commanded. She obeyed like a small child being undressed. He tossed the panty hose aside. "Now get in the water, Abigail."

"Ryan?"

"Yes, they would have shaved her, but her hair will grow back. Now get in." He kneeled beside the tub, took a bar of soap and unwrapped it, then began slowly to soap her arms, rubbing with the cloth as if he were trying to make her blood flow under the skin.

"I can wash myself," she protested, but she did not want him to stop. His touch was rhythmic and soothing.

"Can you?" he asked in an odd voice. Then she was leaning back with her head against the back of the tub, her eyes closed and his hands moving over her body with a soothing warmth that left her feeling lethargic and weak.

"You'll get all wet," she mumbled.

"That would be a tragedy," he said soberly and she heard herself laugh, then her eyes opened wide and she thought, How can I laugh with Trish lying in that hospital?

Then it was tears.

He took her out of the tub and wrapped her in a giant towel, murmuring something formless in her ear and carrying her into the other room. "Sorry," she choked, "I—I wasn't going to cry."

He caught the wet strands of her hair away from her face and slipped the towel between the dampness and her shoulders. She opened her eyes and realized that he had settled into the big armchair near the window with her in his arms, all wrapped in a towel.

"I'm sorry," she whispered, wishing she could just melt back into his arms. Her face was wet from tears, but her arms were trapped in the towel and she knew that she must look a mess and all the worry was in his eyes, too. What right had she to be the one crying and asking him for comfort?

"I'm such a wuss," she said unsteadily. "I'm sorry."

He combed the hair away from her face. "What's a wuss?"

"I don't know." She choked and knew it would not be laughter, but tears again. "Something Trish called her principal, and it feels like it would fit *me* now. I— she won't die, will she?" She blinked and he bent to kiss her eyes where the tears were determined to escape.

"It's all right," he said in an odd voice. "Of course you have to cry. Cry for both of us, and let me hold you... and she'll be all right. In the morning, she'll be awake and it will be all right."

Her body shuddered and she choked off the sound of a sob. He drew her closer in his arms and kissed her face where the tears were lying. The trembling rose up in her as the tears began to flow unhindered. He held her close against him as her sobs faded to silence.

When she was quiet in his arms, he carried her over to one of the two big beds, lay down with her and pulled the spread over them both. She drifted in his arms, her eyes tightly closed, her heart sheltering in his warmth. Finally, she slept, her body tangled in his arms and the tears dried on her face.

CHAPTER TEN

IT WAS dark when she woke. She turned to the warmth beside her, but her seeking hand found only cool emptiness. Abruptly, she sat up, her heart pounding.

Trish!

"Abby?" Ryan's voice was quiet and firm. She felt her whole being turning to focus on it.

A shadow, rising from the easy chair by the window. Last night, he had carried her out of the bath, had held her in his arms while she lost her battle with the tears. Now he was leaning over her, touching her cheek with cool, firm fingers.

"How do you feel?"

"Trish——"

"I called a few minutes ago. She's stable." He pushed the tangle of hair back from her face gently.

"I'm okay." She pushed the sheet aside and his hand closed over hers, stilling her motion. She whispered, "Stable. I hate that word."

"You should go back to sleep."

She shook her head, trying to pull her hand away from his. "I can't."

"They won't let us see her this early. You'd be sitting in that waiting room until the doctor comes. He'll be in again at eight, the nurse said. Meanwhile they're watching Trish closely and she's stable, which is as much as anyone can expect at this stage."

"Damn you," she whispered. "I want to be with her."

His face impassive, he said, "Take it out on me if you want to."

"I'm sorry, Ryan. I just..."

"I know." He brushed her cheek with his lips, then she was free and he was moving toward the window. "If you're determined not to sleep, I'll order coffee for you." He turned to look back at her, his own body just a silhouette against the city night-lights shining through the window. Perversely, now that he had released her, she wanted to shelter in his arms.

"All right," she agreed. He was staring at her, and when his eyes changed she realized that she was naked beneath the sheets, that her breasts were uncovered. She pulled the sheet high. Last night he had washed her naked body everywhere, had lifted her out of the tub and held her close while he dried her.

"Why don't you have a shower while you're waiting for the coffee?" he suggested.

She could not reply.

"I won't watch," he said, and she did not know if it was amusement or weariness in his voice, but he turned away to the telephone. He must think she was a fool, but with his gaze on her...she could not see his face, only his form with the lights shining behind him, his head bent as he talked quietly on the telephone. If he turned to look at her, his eyes would be only half open, but sharp and cataloging every move she made.

He hung up the telephone and turned to face her. She trembled and he asked wearily, "What do you think I'm going to do to you? Why should you be frightened of me?"

She hugged herself, the sheet crushed against her breasts under her crossed arms. Because she felt vulnerable, her heart exposed. Frightened of what he made her feel. She said almost inaudibly, "Because I feel that you stand back and watch...even your own emotions."

He moved away from the telephone and she tensed, but he crossed to the closet and pulled down his overcoat. He slipped it on and she felt the pain of needing his arms. He said, "It's not such a bad thing, Abby, stepping back from yourself. And right now it's a good thing one of us can, because you're swinging like a seesaw."

She gulped, because it was true. She had never thought she was emotional, certainly not erratic. But last night she had sheltered in his arms, crying and holding close. This morning... how could he look at her and know the swing of her heart and her feelings? And why was he leaving her now, putting his coat on and walking toward that door?

"Where are you going?" she asked, afraid of the answer.

He said wearily, "Out to get some coffee. There's no room service until seven. We may be awake, but the desk clerk was sleeping when I called down." He buttoned his overcoat and added sardonically, "So you'll be able to get into the shower without risking my seeing you."

He opened the door and there could not be much doubt that he thought her a fool. Last night, holding her wet, naked body while she burrowed against him. And this morning, watching her tremble while she held the sheet against herself like armor.

"Abby?" He was halfway through the door.

"What?"

"Don't worry. It's going to be all right."

The insane thing was, she could almost believe he could make it right. Trish, lying unconscious—*stable*—in that hospital across the road. And Ryan, promising her everything would be all right.

As if he needed desperately to believe it himself, she thought with sharp certainty. "Ryan, how much sleep did *you* get?"

"Enough," he said. Then he left.

They had breakfast at a nearby Denny's that was open all night. Ryan had scrambled eggs and toast and he made her eat the same thing, watched her and would not let her leave the table until she had eaten every scrap and drank every drop of her orange juice.

"You make me feel like a child," she said resentfully.

At the hospital, they were told to wait in the waiting room for the doctor to finish examining Trish. Eight o'clock in the morning, the sky just lightening outside. Abby looked down at her own hands locked in her lap.

"I must have spilled orange juice on my skirt," she said, surprised that she would notice a stain on her clothing when Trish's life hung in the balance. Blue denim, she thought. A blue skirt. She wondered what kind of color blue was. Some colors were supposed to be better for healing, for soothing anger. Pink for anger, she thought, remembering a documentary about that once, colors used in treatment of mental patients.

Ryan said, "We'll do something later about a change of clothes for you."

He was leaning back in the uncomfortable seat, his long legs stretched out in front of him. She stared at his legs, too long for the seat. She wished he would crack, shout or scream or get angry so that he could not control it.

"How did you find out Trish was at the hospital? The hotel said you'd gone. Where had you gone?"

"Mexico." She had been right about that, she thought. He added, "At least, I was headed that way."

She looked at the clock, the second hand going around, and knew she could not go on thinking all the time of how Trish could lose this battle. "Tell me how you came to have a place there?" she demanded desperately.

"I'd just spent three months in New York, in the middle of the rat race. Larry had persuaded me it would be a good base, but it wasn't for me. So I went into a travel agency and asked the woman there what was the other extreme from New York. She figured that would be the Baja, and I went down there just for a holiday."

He closed his eyes and she could see the weariness in his face. "Most of the Baja is desert, but Todos Santos was so green and lush, palm trees growing everywhere and sandy beaches that stretch on forever."

It was helping him, too, talking. She asked, "When?"

"About six years ago." His hands were clasped loosely, his forearms resting on his thighs as he leaned forward. He was too long for these chairs. A big man who needed big furniture. "I started doing a series of photos on Mexico—not the cities and the tourist spots like Cabo San Lucas and Cozumel, but the little villages and the ranches. Scattering of tourists camping along the beaches, between cowboys and farm workers and street vendors. I picked up the beach house and used it as a base."

She said, "It was a wonderful book, the one on Mexico." She had not let herself buy it, but she had stood in the book store staring at it, turning the pages and feeling Ryan beside her, seeing the world through his eyes. The shopkeeper had come up, speaking enthusiastically about Ryan Marsdon's photo studies and telling Abby they had two other Marsdon books in stock. Abby had closed the cover and put the book carefully back on the shelf. She had left the shop and walked out, had driven to pick Trish up from Sarah's, and it had been days before she could rid herself of the aching feeling of loneliness.

She had only dared buy the one book of his, the one with her name on the dedication. She had known she must never buy another. His pictures had much the same effect on her as the man. It was like a sickness, looking through his lens and feeling him close and knowing that only one man could ever reach through into the core of Abigail Stakeman.

Ryan was telling her about the combers, the big waves that came in south of Todos Santos when the storms came, describing how the young Mexican men took their girlfriends out there in summertime, how the couples ran out into the water, standing motionless to wait for the giant, rolling combers. How the men would catch their girls close as the waves rolled in over them, lost together for a moment in the violence of the sea, coming up a moment later tumbled, dripping water, tight in each other's arms. Abby remembered him holding her close as the water rolled over them.

Then the neurosurgeon came in.

Abby was on her feet, shocked out of listening to a description of Mexican lovers, shaken and guilty that she had actually smiled and almost laughed when Trish was so near death.

"Is she——?" She could not ask, but Ryan's arm was around her and he was saying, "Take it easy, honey," and then she could see that the surgeon's eyes were not hesitating to meet hers, that he had not come to bring the terrible news that would end it all.

Dr. Carridine said, "We've moved your daughter into Intensive Care."

Abby tensed and Ryan asked, "Is that a normal development?"

"Yes, quite normal in these cases." The neurosurgeon pushed a hand through his gray hair and explained, "We kept her in the post-anesthetic recovery room overnight—a matter of available beds, really. She's remained relatively stable, so earlier this morning we moved her into ICU where she can continue to be monitored on a continual basis."

"Is she conscious yet?" asked Ryan.

"No. We wouldn't expect her to regain consciousness for some hours yet. Perhaps not until tomorrow. All I can tell you is that her vitals indicate that the pressure is increasing very slowly."

"Increasing . . ." breathed Abby.

"We've only *relieved* the pressure," explained the surgeon. "To give the injury time to heal itself. The bleeding has slowed, as indicated by the relative stability of her vital signs. All we can do now is wait, and monitor her carefully."

"Can we see her?" asked Ryan, his thumb rubbing against Abby's upper arm in reassurance.

"For twenty minutes," he agreed. "She's unconscious, and there's really nothing you can do for her at this point except wait. After you've seen her, I'd suggest you—you're not local, are you?"

Abby shook her head and Ryan said, "From Maple Bay, but we're staying at a motel nearby."

"Then go off and get some rest again. These things are very exhausting. Spend some time with your daughter, then go outside and have some fresh air, or some more sleep, because I know you couldn't have had much last night."

"No," agreed Ryan, his gaze on Abby, and she wondered exactly how much sleep he had managed to get. Enough, he had said.

A nurse appeared to take them to Trish. Walking behind the white uniform, with Ryan's hand enclosing hers, Abby whispered, "I don't know how I could have slept last night, while Trish..."

The nurse stopped at a room with a glass wall. Through the glass, Abby could see a bed and a motionless form lying covered with white. The nurse said quietly, "It's the best thing you could do for her, getting a good rest yourself." She opened the door and nodded to Ryan.

Abby went to the bed, Ryan at her side. She stared down at her daughter's white face and tried to tell herself that her color was better than it had been last night. She had no idea if it was true or not. Trish's head was swathed in white bandages. Her lips were slack around some plastic device that had been put in her mouth.

Abby trembled and whispered, "Can't she breathe?"

The nurse said calmly, "It's an airway, to keep her tongue from blocking off her breathing while she's unconscious."

Ryan brought a chair from somewhere and Abby sat, wanting to take Trish's hand but unable to because of the tubes going to her arm. Intravenous. And beside the bed, one of those monitors you saw on television when people were on the verge of death in a hospital. A sob rose up in her and she suppressed it, her shoulders stiffening. She put her hand on Trish's upper arm. Her daughter's skin felt slack and lifeless under her touch, but warm. She could feel Ryan behind her, his hands resting on her shoulders as if to give her the quiet strength he seemed to have in such abundance. She reached up and covered one of his hands with one of hers.

Twenty minutes. It seemed forever, watching Trish and listening to the sound of the monitor. Forever, until the nurse came back into the room, then Ryan was urging her to her feet and she could feel the damned tears starting again.

"When can we see her again?" asked Abby stiffly.

"Not for another four hours," the nurse said kindly. "Go off and get some sleep. She's doing quite well, considering."

"Considering?" echoed Abby when they were alone again. Her fingers curled around Ryan's tightly. "What does 'considering' mean?"

Ryan transferred her grip to his other hand so that he could put his arm around her. "It means that every minute she remains stable is a better chance she'll be fine." He was leading her down the corridor and she followed mechanically. Then he was holding her coat and she could not even remember taking it off, but he was helping her into it, turning her, doing up the buttons. He had stayed in his overcoat all along, and she remembered him saying he did not like winter much and thinking that must be another reason why he had bought a place down in Mexico.

"I can't go and sleep," she said dully.

"I know." He fastened the last button and slipped the strap of her bag over her shoulder. "We'll go out and see about buying you a change of clothes."

"I can't go shopping." She pulled back from his hand, said, "I want to stay here." She started toward the waiting room. There were four people there, standing silent and grim, and Abby stopped in the entrance to the room.

"You need to get away," Ryan insisted quietly at her shoulder.

She turned and faced him. He looked calm, and in that moment she hated him for his reasonable control. He said quietly, "You won't do her any good at all, sitting out here in that waiting room, worrying yourself sick. All we can do is wait, and try to stay sane."

She clenched her hands into fists. He took one fist and worked the fingers loose. She stared down at his hand, watching it manipulating hers, and she spat, "Damn you! Do you think I'm some kind of lump?" She heard a sob escape her throat.

"Do you think you're the only one who cares about her?" For just a second his eyes were haunted, his face gray and strained. "If there was anything I could do——" He shrugged and she could feel the tension welling through his body in waves. Then it was gone and he was quiet again, while she was still shuddering from the violence that had blazed in him only a second ago. She remembered last night, Ryan whispering that she must cry for him too, and understood then the pain he was holding inside.

He said with quiet certainty, "All we can do is wait, and think of her as well, not let her lose ground in our minds." His gaze penetrated hers, as if his will could control her thoughts and her feelings.

"Positive thinking?" she asked unsteadily. "Do you think she'll get better just from our believing she will?"

"I've seen stranger things."

She wanted to believe it. She tried to imagine Trish alive, running down the beach to the water, but all she could see was the face of the doctor who had come to her in that London hospital, tired and regretful and telling her that Ben was gone.

Ryan said, "It's the only thing in our power to do, so it's what we *must* do. Part of it is keeping on with the ordinary things, getting you some clothes and a toothbrush."

She had brushed her teeth with a rough facecloth that morning, but it seemed wrong to think about anything so mundane as needing a toothbrush. She said tightly, "You want me to leave Trish?"

"Damn it, Abby! We're not leaving her. She's at the other end of that corridor, and they're not going to let us see her again for hours. Time, and waiting. You heard Dr. Carridine. Go away, get some rest. There's nothing we can do right now."

She glared at him, her breath coming hard and fast. "You have no right to try to tell me how to handle this."

"Yes, I do," he retorted, his voice hard and angry, too. "You're not looking after yourself, not letting anyone else, and by the time Trish opens her eyes you're going to be a damned wreck if somebody doesn't make you look after yourself. I'm not going to let it happen."

"You think you can stop me?"

"Yes," he said, and she stepped back from the tone in his voice. He ground out, "You have a hell of a way of handling disasters, and I'm not going to let you turn into the kind of mess you were when I met you in London. You force yourself to stay awake, to keep everything locked up, and the next thing you know you'll be wandering into some gallery half out of your mind and I'm not having you end up in some other man's bed because you can't look after yourself."

She jerked as if he had slapped her. "You—I——"

Suddenly, the anger seemed to drain out of him. He caught both her hands and pulled her toward him. "I'm sorry! I—for God's sake, Abby, just let me look after you."

There must have been tears in her eyes because he brushed them away. She whispered, "I didn't think you understood. About London."

"I understand now," he said.

She swallowed. "It was...I—I never before felt the way I felt with you that day." She closed her eyes, opened them abruptly again because she could feel the tears there. "If Trish..."

"We'll call every half hour," he promised. "And don't bother coming up with any more arguments, because I'm not listening to them." She bit her lip, staring at him, and he said gently, "Now will you come with me?"

"All right." Of course it made sense. Just sitting, worrying, was enough to drive anyone insane. Doing something made it easier. Easier to believe that Trish would pull through, walking along the pavement with Ryan's hand closed over hers and the sun slipping up in the sky.

"What do you want?" he asked. "An expensive ladies' wear shop? Or a department store?" She shrugged, but he would not let her get away with that. "Do you want jeans and a shirt? Or a dress?"

"I don't care."

"You'd better," he said, stopping short of the rank of taxis. "Because we're not getting in the taxi until you've made some kind of decision. What sort of clothes do you want to buy?"

"Are you working on my mental health?"

"Yes," he said simply.

She sighed and incredibly her lips twitched. "Jeans, then. *And* a dress."

He nodded. "Good. Which store? You know this city better than I." He smiled wryly. "Especially when it comes to ladies' wear."

"Eaton's," she decided. "I can get everything there."

He nodded and finally led her to the taxi. When the driver was moving his car smoothly through the early morning quiet, she sat quietly beside Ryan, wishing that he would hold her hand again. He was leaning back on the other end of the seat, his thigh just brushing against her skirt.

If he ever asked her to marry him again, she would say yes. He probably would not ask, because she had run out on promises to him twice now. In London, when he had waited at the gallery for her to meet him. And yesterday—was it only yesterday?—sitting across from him, telling him she could not marry him although she had promised.

She knew it was the way he was made, that he would always be separate from the emotions, even when they were his. It was probably the thing that made him an incredibly good photographer, seeing the world from outside while he was inside himself. Except with Trish, because he was hurting inside, worried about his daughter. But for the rest of the world, he watched through a camera lens, watched her through a camera lens. He cared about her. Of course he did, or he would not be taking so much trouble now, trying to keep her sane and putting up with... with everything.

He cared, but Ryan would never be a headlong, out-of-control lover. She studied the back of the driver's head, Ryan's dark shape lying in her peripheral vision, and knew it was impossible to ask a man to be someone else. She might ache all her life for him to give back the shattering depth of love she felt. Her only choice, really, was either to ache alone, or try life with him at her side.

The driver said something, and she closed her eyes, listening to Ryan talking with the driver about the proposal for a new Pat Bay highway through the Victoria area. She wondered if he would ever ask her to belong to him again. She would say yes, but what would happen if one day she lost the little bit of control she had maintained with him? What if she held tightly to him and begged him to love her, to need her, to ache for her and make her whole?

"...not open for another half hour," Ryan was saying to her. "We'll have a coffee first." He leaned forward and his shoulder brushed against Abby as he spoke to the driver. "Could you let us off at a quiet coffee shop close to the Eaton's store?"

He would always be the controlled one, organized and practical. That made a crazy kind of nonsense, because he was the artist, showing other people how to look at the world with his camera. He paid the driver and held the door of the coffee shop for her, helped her out of her coat and made small talk with the waitress who greeted them. He ordered her coffee and sat down across from her when he had shed his own coat.

She watched his hands moving, arranging the things on the table between them. He got calmer in a crisis. She kept her gaze on his hands and said pensively, "I always thought I wasn't an emotional person."

One of his hands reached across and took hers. "Anyone can see you're seething with emotions inside. Boiling with feeling. You just get tangled up sometimes, unable to let it out."

Tangled up. It was an apt description of the way she felt. About him. About Trish. About herself. "And afraid of my own feelings," she said, and was glad he made no comment about that, because she had not meant to say it. She grimaced. "You're telling me I need a shrink?"

"No." He turned her hand up, examined the lines on her palm. "But you're the only person who's ever been able to see into me."

"I can't see anything." She shook her head to emphasize that. "Sometimes I feel as if you're hidden behind a mask."

He said with quiet mockery, "A man trapped behind a mask. But you see through it when you look. We'd better make a list of what you need." He had out paper and pen and it was typical that he had changed the subject so quickly.

"Organizing me again?" she asked wryly. "I'm supposed to be the organized one. I'm the accountant." He had let go of her hand when he reached for his pen and she pulled her hand back abruptly, because he might think she wanted him to hold it again.

"You're an unlikely accountant, Abigail, but it will do until you realize that you were meant to be an artist." Her lips parted in protest and he said, "Toothpaste? No, you can use mine. Toothbrush. Hairbrush?"

"You do that all the time." She picked up the steaming cup of coffee that had appeared at her elbow without her noticing. "You say something penetrating, then you sidestep before I can react. As if——"

His brows were raised and he said gently, "I told you that you could see through me. Jeans? Blouse? Underthings?"

"Things?" Her lips twitched, then she flushed at the look in his eyes. "You didn't tell me how you got my message. Did you phone your agent? I left a message on his service."

"No. What about makeup?" So he was not going to tell her. She frowned and he said, "Ask me another time. I might tell you. What else will you need?"

"A nightgown." She dropped her gaze to her coffee cup, flushing. Would they share the same room again tonight? She was mostly rational now, and he might decide she did not need twenty-four-hour care. She said hesitantly, "It's—wouldn't the store be open by now?" and wondered if she had the nerve to ask him to stay with her, to tell him she needed his arms around her?

"Let's go, then," he said, and put his cup down.

"Where's your camera?" He had not been wearing it when he came to her in the hospital. Had not brought it with them this morning. She could not remember ever seeing him without it for so long.

"In my luggage," he said, shrugging the question away, turning to claim her coat. Evading her eyes, she thought, and wondered what it was that he could not let her see. She went outside while he was paying the bill, waiting for him, turning to him as he came through the door, her hand reached toward his. He stared down at her for a second, his eyes blank, and she pulled her hand back and stuffed it into her coat pocket.

"Did you phone?" she asked. She had seen him reaching for the pay telephone on the wall as he turned away from the cashier.

"Yes. There's no change."

She nodded, taking in a deep breath. "I left my car in the drop-off lane at the hospital back in Duncan."

"Don't worry about it. I'll look after it."

"They might tow it away."

He shrugged. "If so, I'll look after that, too."

Every minute gave Trish a better chance, he had said. She bit her lip, turned and said, "Eaton's is this way. Or should I go on my own, and you can meet me in half an hour?"

He went with her.

She picked up a pair of jeans from a rack, added a blouse and turned to the cashier. "No," he said. "Try them on. You'd try them on normally, wouldn't you?"

"Yes." If they pretended everything was going to be all right, would it come true? Or was it just a way to keep sane while they waited? Normal, except that every thirty minutes they reached for a telephone.

* * *

"You can look in for just a minute," said the nurse when they arrived back at the hospital. "She's still unconscious, but Dr. Carridine was quite pleased when he saw her twenty minutes ago. He'll be around soon, I expect, to talk to you."

Abby's gaze went to Ryan's eyes. She reached for his hand and he curled his fingers around hers as they walked together toward the intensive care unit.

"Her color *is* better," whispered Abby.

Ryan said, "Yes," and she thought it was true. She could see the rise and fall of Trish's chest, definite breathing. If it had not been for the beep of the monitor and the mess of life-saving tubes and equipment all around her, Trish might have been sleeping normally.

Ryan moved toward the window and leaned against it. Watching over me, Abby thought, and watching over Trish. She blinked and suddenly believed he was right about *thinking* Trish better, because Abby could close her eyes and see Trish laughing and running, looking at her mother with that confusing restraint that came to her so easily. Except that since Ryan had come into their lives Trish seemed much less restrained.

Dr. Carridine slipped into the room, picked up the chart from the foot of Trish's bed and murmured something indistinct to Abby and Ryan. Abby watched as he moved to Trish's head, turned back her eyelids one at a time and examined her eyes intently. Then he stood motionless, eyes off in space, while he held her wrist and felt her pulse. That must be for effect, Abby thought, because the monitor was beeping regularly, broadcasting Trish's heartbeat for everyone to hear.

"Eyes look stable," he murmured. "Dilating equally. We may be winning here." His gaze swept the two people staring at him. "All right if you want to stay for a bit...half an hour, then go off, leave her alone for a few hours."

He left as quietly as he had come, with a silent, white-clad nurse in his wake. Ryan drew in a haggard breath and pushed himself away from the window. "Did he say...winning?"

Abby breathed in shakily. "Yes."

Twenty minutes later, Trish's eyes fluttered.

Abby leaned forward and touched her daughter's arm.

Ryan moved to the other side of the bed, pressed the buzzer that would bring the nurse with one hand, while he placed the other lightly on Trish's shoulder and said, "Hello, Trish. You've had a long sleep."

Trish blinked and rolled her head, her mouth moving, fighting the airway. Then the nurse was bending over her, slipping the plastic device away, saying briskly, "We're just fine, dear. Now what's your name?"

Trish stared at her blankly, her eyelids starting to crawl back over her eyes. "Come on, dear," the nurse insisted. "What's your name?"

"Trish. Patricia...what happened to the kitten?"

"What kitten?" asked Abby, touching her daughter's face and feeling the tears on her own. "What kitten, honey?"

Trish's eyes were closed, her voice murmuring indistinctly, "Was on the roof...crying, and I had to... but...then...ran away."

Abby thought she was asleep again, but Ryan said, "Don't worry about the kitten, honey. I'll find out for you," and Trish's eyes fluttered briefly.

CHAPTER ELEVEN

As THE door to her motel room closed behind her, Abby turned and faced it, her lips parted, eyes wide. Ryan was not there. He had ushered her into the room, shut the door and left himself outside.

She turned back and swept the motel room with her eyes. Ryan made a habit of doing that, she thought. Making her think he was about to reach for her, just before he pulled away. She grimaced and admitted she was not much better. And this time, he could easily have decided he'd had enough of baby-sitting Abby Stakeman. He could be in that room across the corridor thanking his luck that she had turned him down, that he was not doomed to have her clinging to him for the rest of his life.

The bed that had not been slept in was littered with the results of their shopping trip that morning. The other bed, the one he had lain in with her through part of last night, was only slightly rumpled. That afternoon Ryan had insisted she come back to the motel for a few hours' rest before the evening visiting hours. Trish had been declared officially out of danger and moved from the intensive care unit into a private room.

Abby had agreed to go to the motel for some sleep, hoping he would rest, too. She had lain on top of the spread fully dressed, pretending to sleep while Ryan sat in a nearby chair reading a magazine. She must have actually fallen asleep, though, because she had opened her eyes and the room had been dark with the day's end. Ryan had been sleeping, too, sitting up in the chair with his head leaned back and the magazine fallen to the floor by his feet.

She had got up and gone to him then, had touched his arm softly. His head had jerked up, his eyes open and staring. Neither of them had said anything, staring at each other through the dark, although Abby's heart had stopped as if they were saying words that meant forever and together.

Then he had pushed her hand away and stood up, had glanced at his watch and pushed the button to light the dial. "I think I'll have a shower before we go to supper," he had said coolly. "By that time, it should be time for visiting hours."

When they got to the hospital, they found Trish sitting up in bed, her head swathed in white and her voice clear. "What about the kitten?" she demanded immediately.

Abby had bit her lip guiltily. She had forgotten the kitten entirely, but Ryan had answered, "I phoned around, and it belongs to the people in the big red house behind the school grounds. It's safely back home now."

Trish had relaxed then, announcing, "They shaved my head. I'll need a wig to go back to school."

Abby had been the one pacing this time, moving restlessly around the room while Ryan sat in a chair near the bed and Trish's conversation slowly faded as her gaze drooped. "Mr. Donnell will be mad at me," she had announced quietly.

"Donnell?" Ryan's eyebrows rose.

"The principal," volunteered Abby. "According to Trish, he's either a quad or a wuss—and I suspect Trish has it right."

Her daughter looked quietly smug. "I *knew* you didn't like him."

Abby turned at the window, leaning against the wide, low sill and watching her daughter, wondering why she could never see her thoughts. "About school, Trish—if you want to change, you can. You don't want to take the extra art courses now, so you could go back to the local school."

Trish sat up, her hand going to the bandage. Ryan moved as if to protect her from what must be a very sore head. Trish bit her lip and said with quiet intensity, "I want to take drama from Mrs. Calliwell next term," and her green eyes went black with emotion.

"Drama...?" Abby shook her head in confusion.

Trish wailed, "Mom——!"

Ryan touched Trish's hand. "Settle down, kiddo. Your mom's not about to haul you away to another school if you want to stay. If you want drama, I'm sure you can have drama." Abby thought he was amused, perhaps because he could see how stunned Abby was at the news that her daughter had developed a passionate interest in drama.

Passionate, under that cool exterior. Abby shook her head, wondering if she would ever know Trish. All those years, Hans had been pushing art and Trish had not complained. As if she had not cared one way or the other, until lately when she had started her quiet rebellion of passive resistance.

"Drama," muttered Abby as she left the hospital with Ryan. "How could anyone as reserved as Trish want to get up on stage in front of everyone? I'm never going to understand her."

Ryan chuckled, taking her arm to steer her toward the crosswalk, toward the motel. "A lot of famous actors are very private, very shy people," he said. "It doesn't stop them from needing to get up on stage."

Abby nodded, knowing he was right, but still confused by the daughter who seemed to be a stranger, but not a stranger. She felt Ryan's hand on her arm, knew that she belonged to him no matter what else happened. Then she turned and walked with him toward the motel.

"Don't worry," he told her. "If she's meant for life on the stage, she'll find out for herself. We'll just give her the opportunities, let her grow into the woman she wants to be."

"Yes," she agreed. "Will you help me tell her?"

"Tell her what?"

"That you're her father."

His eyes shuttered. "You're sure you want to?" She nodded, and he said gently, "Yes, then. Of course I will." He brushed a strand of hair back behind her ear. "Don't worry. It'll be all right."

She believed him.

But then he had stopped at the desk and rented a second room for himself, and he'd moved his bags out of the room they had shared, pushed her through the door and smiled at her as if she were a stranger. The last thing he'd said to her was, "Get a good rest."

Alone.

Abby glanced at the door again now, feeling angry and knowing she was doing it again. Reacting, being emotional, swinging from anger to...to love, and back again, and not knowing the whole time where she really stood. She began to pull the morning's shopping out of the bags, piling the litter into the small waste bin with furious intensity, putting the silky lingerie into the dresser, the dress on a hanger in the cupboard.

She put the new nightgown over the chair where Ryan had sat to read, because she might as well have a shower and go to bed. She did not feel tired, but she would pull up the covers and turn on the television and watch until she got sick of it or fell asleep.

She made the shower warm, because it was cold outside. She used the new shampoo on her hair and the

new bar of scented soap on her body. Last night Ryan
had washed her with the motel's soap, taking the paper
wrapper off and sudsing her body carefully, touching
her without any sexual overtones although she remembered looking up once and seeing his eyes all dark and
opaque.

As they had the night when he made love to her on
Quadra Island. And other times. So many times. She
turned the water off and it all streamed down her body,
making little water beads on her skin while her hair lay
heavy and wet around her shoulders.

She would not need toothpaste, he had said, because
she could use his. But he was not here. He was in the
room across the hall, but when he'd told her not to buy
toothpaste he must have intended to be with her tonight.

Then he had changed his mind. But why?

Ryan always worked things out, watched, did not make
that kind of careless mistake. She pushed the water down
her naked skin with her hands sliding along her midriff,
her abdomen, her hips. She stared at the door she had
not closed, wondered if she would have left it open if
he had been in the room beyond, thought she might have
if she had the nerve.

She was terrified. And she was definitely a wuss, because she had no courage at all. She stepped out of the
tub and reached for the towel, wrapped it around herself
and went into the bedroom, her wet feet making marks
on the carpet. She dried herself and wrapped a dry towel
around, tucking it in at the front of her breasts to anchor
it. Then she picked up the new hair drier and brushed
her hair to sleek golden softness while she dried it. She
put her glasses on and frowned at herself in the mirror,
wishing for once that she had the contact lenses with her
because she wanted to look as good as she possibly could,
but she needed to see, to watch.

He had said she could see though his mask if she tried. That day in London, she had seen him leaning back, watching, had known that he had taken those harsh pictures with hot emotion hidden somewhere deep inside.

On Quadra Island, when he began to make love to her, she had reached for him, needing to have him with her when she lost control, and her memory could not be so hazed with the echo of passion that she was wrong. He had been with her. There had been no cool watcher in her arms that night.

Not until the next morning, when he made coffee for her and suggested they get married as if it were the kind of thing people should do when they shared a child. For Trish. For compatibility. Not for love.

She put on makeup. Lipstick and eye shadow and mascara. Too much, she thought, and scrubbed it all off again. She opened the drawer and studied the little pile of lingerie. Panty hose? Should she wear the jeans and one of the blouses she had bought? If so, she would go barefoot, but if she wore the dress she should have panty hose and shoes.

She bit her lip and saw her face in the mirror, her eyes wide behind the glasses. She should put the makeup back on. Makeup, clothes—armor, to protect herself. If that was the way she was going to do it, she might as well stay here and watch television. She pulled off the towel, dropped it to the carpet and reached for the nightgown.

It was not exactly transparent. Sleeveless, it hung in a deceptively simple line from her shoulders, dropping to mid-thigh with a simplicity that disappeared when she moved. When she walked, the satiny fabric moved sensuously over her body.

Ryan had picked it out, reaching it down from a rack of silky finery as if it were the only item there. An intimate thing, buying a seductive nightgown for a woman.

She had paid for the jeans and the dress, the hair drier and the makeup, but he had bought the nightgown for her.

She opened the door and stepped out into the corridor, telling herself that it did not make sense. Why should Ryan have to marry her when he knew he could see all he wanted of Trish? He had certainly had no need to seduce her, and, as to that, he had been as far gone in love and passion as she had.

Love?

That was what she was reaching for, frightened of, because what if she was wrong about the things she thought she had seen in his eyes? It was all very fine to reason it out, but she had never pretended to be strong on logic once she got outside the office. Maybe Ryan was right and she would make a better artist than an accountant, although the thought of her drawings on exhibition gave her the shudders, panic almost as severe as what she felt staring at the door to his room. Maybe she could do the art thing if he stood beside her. Alone, she wasn't sure.

Here she was, out in the corridor, on his doorstep. But what was she going to do when she knocked and he answered? What was she going to say? "You said you would come to claim me. All right, how about now?" She shook her head, staring at the door to his room, lifting her hand and letting it fall back. Something more straightforward. "Why don't we get married? You suggested it and you got the license and is two days up on Sunday or do they not count Sundays?"

She knocked once, pulled her hand back. If he . . . he might not have heard that knock. She could turn and go back and there would be nothing lost except that she would be exactly where she had started.

Someone turned the corner at the end of the corridor and she glanced back at the safety of her own room, only she had closed the door as she came out and it was one of those doors that locked itself every time it was closed.

Then Ryan opened the door. She bit her lip, knowing she had been wrong to think she could do this, come up with words. He had one hand stretched across the entrance to his room, blocking her way as he watched her.

"Ryan? Would you... let me in? I've locked myself out."

He opened the door wider. She went in. From behind her, she heard him close the door. He said, "I thought you would run away again. I certainly didn't expect you at my door." She turned to face him. He was standing very still, watching her. He said, "You've run from me often enough, I could hardly help knowing that I throw you into a panic."

"I'm done running." She wanted to touch him, thought it would be easier if they could touch.

"Oh?"

"I shouldn't have said I would marry you. Not then." Something jerked in his jaw and she explained, "You made it so complicated." Trish and the knowledge that he would be around always, that she could not escape seeing him, being near him. The knowledge inside that she did not want to escape, that anything she could have of him must be better than the void of nothing.

He had made his face a mask. He had told her she could see through, but she saw only careful blankness in his eyes. Then he said, "I thought if we made love again that it would hold you." He shrugged as if it did not matter. "I was wrong. It put you further away."

She whispered, "You could have bonded me with words," and something happened in his eyes. She tried to get breath into her lungs. She had no courage for this. She whispered, "You could have told me you loved me."

He shook his head and she felt something curling up in agony inside herself. He gestured to the desk behind her and she turned to look. Pictures were scattered everywhere, but she could not focus on them. No camera today or yesterday, but in here, pictures everywhere. She moved slowly toward them.

He said, "When you walked out of that restaurant on Friday, I thought I would never come back. You asked me how I got your message and I'll tell you. When you walked out of the restaurant, I left that town forever. I checked out of my hotel, took back the rental car. I made reservations to get as far away as I could—that's the second time I've done that, you know, and it was no different this time from the last."

She whispered, "What do you mean?"

He was standing beside her, staring down at the pictures. She could not see his face. He said grimly, "I tried to leave after that exhibition. I couldn't. And this time, it took me about an hour to realize that no matter what I'd always have to come back to you." She could only see the side of his face, his jaw clenched tightly as he ground out the words one by one, separately and intensely. "If it can't be marriage, I guess I can accept that. But I've got to be in your life. There has to be some way we can be together."

She whispered, "Ryan," and he stood straight, facing her so that she saw the pain in his eyes.

He said harshly, "If it's time you need, than I'll give you whatever time I can. I can't promise I'll be patient, because patient is the last thing I can feel when I'm around you—when I'm looking at the rest of my life and seeing it empty and black without you."

She was trembling so badly that she could hardly speak. She looked down at the pictures of herself. Pictures of a woman in love, taken by a man...a man in love with the woman he saw through the lens? It showed with every click of his shutter.

She heard the harsh air tearing through his lungs. "Abby, maybe it's never been what you've wanted, but I've loved you from the first moment I saw you." He laughed harshly and paced away from her, spun back and said angrily, "I know that's damned nonsense. I spent years telling myself it was crazy, that you were just a woman who had walked across my life, that you were nothing but memory, that a man could not love a woman when he didn't even know her damned name!"

She was trembling, her gaze riveted on his back. Any second she would get her legs to move, would go to him and touch him and tell him she loved him. He spun around again, facing her, glaring at her, his mouth a grim line, his eyes hot with fury and something perhaps nearer hate than love. He said harshly, "I found you again, and you were the woman in my dreams."

Pain in his voice. She reached for him and he did not come.

"I learned of you again this year. Abigail, not Gail, but I had always known you. Always loved you." His jaw jerked with words suppressed and he finished grimly, "You can hardly pretend you don't feel the force of what's between us, but it's obviously not what you— damn it, Abigail! Somehow—there's got to be some way for us!"

He could not stay still, any more than she could move. He came just two steps away from her, just out of reach of her outstretched hand, said harshly, "You told me to stay away from you, but I can't. You've haunted me for twelve years, and now I'm going to haunt you."

She whispered his name, but he could not hear. He held her eyes and promised grimly, "For the rest of your life, if it takes that long. You won't be able to turn around without finding me there. I'll buy the house next to yours, I'll be at your door every night. Every time you turn around, you'll find me waiting for you." His eyes drove into hers. "And one day I'll claim you."

She managed to say, "You said that before. About claiming me."

"Yes, I did. This time, there will be no more running away."

"I told you I was done with running." She wondered if he could feel her heart crashing against her ribs. "And you're the one who keeps moving. One day, you'll leave."

"Only if you come with me."

She felt her heart beating heavier, swelling with love and the knowledge of the tomorrows they would have. She said, "Claiming me... you could do it now."

"When you're ready," he promised. "Because there will be no escape, Abby. It will be forever. You asked me why I'd never married—only one reason. Because none of the women were you."

She moved closer to him, put both palms flat on his chest and felt the slow, heavy thud of his heartbeat. "Last time," she said, "I asked you why you wanted to marry me. You said for Trish. And that we were compatible. As if—— Why didn't you tell me you loved me?"

His eyes narrowed and she thought the shutters might have begun to close over the flames, then he said quietly, "I was afraid. Sick with the fear that I would have to watch you turn away from me." His voice turned harsh again, but she could see through his haggard face, could hear the love and pain. "Know this, Abigail. It might be crazy, but I've loved you since before the first time

I saw you, and it's not going to go away. And one day, somehow, you're going to love me too."

"Yesterday," she promised, spreading her hands out, sliding them to curve around his shoulders, to hold herself close and feel his tension snapping between them. "And today. And forever." Her lips were parted and she whispered softly, "If you want me, then claim me, but if you start talking about practical reasons for us being together again so help me I'll put poison in your coffee."

She opened her eyes, found his wide and staring down at her, delving deep for the truth. She was very still, to let him see inside her heart, her soul. She said unevenly, "All those years... since London—I would wake from dreams of you, and I would feel as if it were the dream that was real, that I would be alone forever without you. That memory of you... you and I—was beyond anything else I've ever experienced. And——"

He took her lips carefully, then more deeply as he felt her tremble and cling to him. When she was breathless, he carefully slid her glasses off.

"You've gone fuzzy," she said in a shaken voice.

"I'll fix that," he promised, drawing her close with shattering intimacy.

She pressed even closer against him, felt his body respond and his hands harden on her back, sliding down the satiny fabric to form her hips lovingly. She trembled and he throbbed against her. She said, "I knew when I saw you in that gallery in Victoria. I'd have known you anywhere. From the front, from the back. Running away. My heart recognized you."

He swung her up into his arms. She held tightly to his neck, burying her face against his throat as he carried her, pressing her lips against his pulse and feeling his hard body tremble at her caress. Then she was sinking down, looking up and seeing his face vulnerable, filled with love for her.

He said, "I told myself I would tear that marriage license up, that it was nothing but a piece of paper. But I've still got it. It's in my wallet." His eyes probed hers and she could see uncertainty behind the question.

"I'd counted on that," she told him, her lips seeking his. She kept her eyes open and she could see the hazel in his turn to blazing amber as their lips touched. She felt his breath go harsh and knew that he had told the truth. She could always penetrate the mask he kept between himself and the world. All she had to do was look.

"I've always loved you," he growled in a shaken voice, taking her close.

"I know," she whispered back, her lips against his. "And I—back in London when I didn't meet you the next day—I told myself it was impossible, that you and I...what had burned up between us—I told myself it was only sexual, a moment of madness that had happened because I was so upset that day. But—what I felt for Ben was really only hero worship, although I didn't admit that to myself for a long time. I'd been hurt so much by him, by dreaming things that just weren't there between Ben and me. And then, meeting you—I tried to hide what I felt for you, hide from myself the knowledge that you had my heart from that first moment in London. I had to run from what had happened to us, because I knew you had the power to destroy me, far more than Ben ever had."

"Or the power to love you," he whispered in a voice that made her heart tremble with happiness. "Don't you know, my darling, that if I hurt you I would be hurting myself far more?"

"Ryan, darling—I love you! Please...please...love me."

He moved his hand in a caress, heating her blood to boiling, turning his own breathing into shuddering passion as he claimed the woman he loved.

"Love me," she whispered, "now."

"Forever," he promised. It was the last coherent thing either of them said for a long time.

POSTCARDS FROM EUROPE

HARLEQUIN PRESENTS

Hi!
Things haven't changed much in Portugal. In fact, Vitor wants to pick up where we left off. But I simply can't let him discover he's the father of my son!
Love, Ashley

HARLEQUIN®

PRESENTS *Plus*

When Cyn discovers that her latest client's future groom is Wolf Thornton, the man *she'd* once intended to marry, she begins to dream about a return engagement.

Laura's fiancé, Patrick, is a true romantic *and* he likes to cook. So why is she falling in love with Josh Kern, a man who is Patrick's complete opposite?

Fall in love with Wolf and Josh—Cyn and Laura do!

Watch for

Return Engagement by Carole Mortimer
Harlequin Presents Plus #1671

and

Falling in Love by Charlotte Lamb
Harlequin Presents Plus #1672

Harlequin Presents Plus
The best has just gotten better!

Available in August wherever Harlequin books are sold.